PENGUIN **MODERN CLASSICS**

STRAIT IS **THE GATE**

André Paul Guillaume Gide was born in Paris on 22
November 1869. His father, who died when he was
eleven, was Professor of Law at the Sorbonne. An only
child, Gide had an irregular and lonely upbringing and
was educated in the Protestant secondary school in
Paris, though his mother's family had recently become
Catholic. He became devoted to literature and music,
and began his literary career as an essayist, and then
went on to poetry, biography, fiction, drama, criticism,
reminiscence and translation. By 1917 he had emerged
as a prophet to French youth and his unorthodox views
were a source of endless debate and attack. In 1947 he
was awarded the Nobel Prize for Literature and in
1948, as a distinguished foreigner, was given an
honorary degree at Oxford. He married his cousin in
1892; he died in Paris in 1951 at the age of eighty-one.
Gide's best known works in England are *Strait is the
Gate* (La Porte Étroite), the first novel he wrote,
which was published in France in 1909; *The Coiners*
(Les Faux-Monnayeurs) published in 1926; and the
famous *Journals* covering his life from 1889 to 1949.

ANDRÉ GIDE

STRAIT IS THE GATE

PENGUIN BOOKS

Penguin Books Ltd, Harmondsworth, Middlesex, England
Viking Penguin Inc., 40 West 23rd Street, New York, New York 10010, U.S.A.
Penguin Books Australia Ltd, Ringwood, Victoria, Australia
Penguin Books Canada Limited, 2801 John Street, Markham, Ontario, Canada L3R 1B4
Penguin Books (N.Z.) Ltd, 182–190 Wairau Road, Auckland 10, New Zealand

—

Strait is the Gate first published as *La Porte Étroite*, Paris 1909
This translation first published by Martin Secker & Warburg Ltd 1924
Published in Penguin Books 1952
Reprinted with *The Vatican Cellars* in Penguin Modern Classics 1965
Reissued as a separate volume in Penguin Modern Classics 1969
Reprinted 1971, 1973, 1974, 1976,
1977, 1979, 1981, 1983, 1985, 1986

—

—

Set, printed and bound in Great Britain by
Cox & Wyman Ltd, Reading
Set in Monotype Bembo

Strive to enter in at the strait gate

LUKE xiii, 24

TO M.A.G.

SOME people might have made a book out of it; but the story I am going to tell is one which took all my strength to live and over which I spent all my virtue. So I shall set down my recollections quite simply, and if in places they are ragged I shall have recourse to no invention, and neither patch nor connect them; any effort I might make to dress them up would take away the last pleasure I hope to get in telling them.

I lost my father before I was twelve years old. As there was nothing to keep my mother at Le Havre, where my father had had a practice as a doctor, she decided to go to Paris where she thought I should be better able to finish my education. She took a small apartment near the Luxembourg and Miss Ashburton came to live with us. Miss Flora Ashburton, who had no relations of her own, had begun by being my mother's governess; she afterwards became her companion and later on her friend. I spent my childhood in the society of these two women whom I remember as equally gentle and equally sad, and always dressed in mourning. One day – it was a good long time, I think, after my father's death – my mother changed the black ribbon in her morning cap for a mauve one.

'Oh, mamma!' I cried. 'That colour doesn't suit you at all.' The next morning the black ribbon was back again.

My health was delicate. My mother and Miss Ashburton had only one thought – to keep me from ailing. If I have not become an idler as a result of their solicitude it must really be that my love of work is ingrained. At the very beginning of the fine weather they both used to persuade themselves that it was time for me to leave town, that I was growing pale. About the middle of June we would start for Fongueusemare, in the neighbourhood of Le Havre, where we used to spend the summer every year at my Uncle Bucolin's.

Standing in a garden which is neither very large nor very fine, and which has nothing special to distinguish it from a number of other Normandy gardens, the Bucolins' house, a white two-storied building, resembles a great many country houses of the century before last. A score of large windows look east on to the front of the garden; as many more on to the back; there are none at the sides. The windows have small panes; some of them, which have been recently replaced, seem too light in colour among the old ones, which look green and dull beside them. Certain others have flaws in the glass which our parents used to call 'bubbles'; a tree seen through them becomes distorted; when the postman passes he suddenly develops a hump.

The garden is rectangular and is enclosed by a wall. The part which lies in front of the house consists of a fairly large, shady lawn with a gravel path all round it. On this side the wall is lower and allows a view of the farmyard and buildings which lie round the garden; the farm is bordered, according to the custom of the country, by an avenue of beeches.

Behind the house on the west side the garden spreads more spaciously. A walk, gay with flowers, runs along the south espalier wall and is protected from the sea winds by a thick screen of Portugal laurel and a few trees. Another walk running along the north wall disappears under a mass of branches. My cousins used to call it the 'dark walk' and would not venture along it after twilight. These two paths led to the kitchen-garden, which continues the flower-garden on a lower level, and which you reach by a small flight of steps. Then, at the bottom of the kitchen-garden, a little gate with a secret fastening leads, on the other side of the wall, to a coppice in which the beech avenue terminates right and left. As one stands on the door-step of the west front one can look over the top of this clump of trees to the plateau beyond with its admirable clothing of crops. On the horizon, at no great distance, can be seen the church of a little village and, when the air is still, the smoke rising from half a dozen houses.

Every fine summer evening after dinner we used to go down

to the 'lower garden'. We went out by the little secret gate and walked as far as a bench in the avenue from which there was a view over the country; there, near the thatched roof of a deserted marl-pit, my uncle, my mother, and Miss Ashburton would sit down; before us the little valley filled with mist, and over the distant woods we watched the sky turn golden. Afterwards we would linger for a while at the lower end of the garden where it had already grown dark. When we came in we found my aunt in the drawing-room. She hardly ever went out with us. For us children the evening ended here; but very often we were still reading in our rooms when we heard our elders go up to bed.

Almost every hour of the day which we did not spend in the garden we spent in the 'school-room', my uncle's study, in which some school desks had been placed for us. My cousin Robert and I worked side by side – behind us were Juliette and Alissa. Alissa was two years older than I, and Juliette one year younger; Robert was the youngest of us four.

I am not writing here an account of my early recollections, but only of those which refer to my story. It really begins, I may say, in the year of my father's death. Perhaps my sensibility – over-stimulated as it has been by our bereavement and if not by my own grief at any rate by the sight of my mother's – predisposed me at this time to new emotions. I had matured precociously, so that when we went to Fongueusemare that year, Juliette and Robert seemed to me all the younger by comparison, but when I saw Alissa I understood on a sudden that we two had ceased to be children.

Yes, it was certainly the year of my father's death; my recollection is confirmed by a conversation which, I remember, took place between my mother and Miss Ashburton immediately after our arrival. I had come unexpectedly into the room where my mother and her friend were talking together; the subject of their talk was my aunt. My mother was indignant that she had not gone into mourning or had gone out again so soon. (To tell the truth it was as impossible for me to imagine Aunt Bucolin dressed in black as my mother in colours.) The day of our arrival Lucile Bucolin, as far as I can remember, was wearing a muslin gown. Miss Ashburton, conciliatory as ever, was trying to calm my mother.

'After all,' she argued timidly, 'white is mourning too.'

'And do you call that red shawl she has round her shoulders mourning too? Flora, I am ashamed of you,' cried my mother.

It was only during the holidays that I saw my aunt and no doubt the warm summer weather was the reason of her wearing the transparent, low-necked bodices in which I always remember her; but still more than the brilliant colour of the scarves which she used to throw over her bare shoulders, it was my aunt's low necks that shocked my mother.

Lucile Bucolin was very beautiful. I still have by me a little portrait of her, in which I can see her as she then was, looking so young that she might have been taken for the elder sister of her daughters, sitting sideways in an attitude which was habitual to her, her head leaning on her left hand, her little finger curved rather affectedly towards her lip. A large-meshed net confines the masses of her curly hair, which fall half-uncoiled upon her neck. In the opening of her bodice a locket of Italian mosaic hangs from a loosely tied black velvet neck ribbon. Her black velvet sash, with its wide floating bow, her broad-brimmed soft straw hat which is dangling from the back of her chair – everything adds to the childishness of her appearance. Her right hand hangs by her side, holding a shut book.

Lucile Bucolin came from a West Indian family: she had either never known her parents or lost them very early. My mother told me later that when she was left an orphan, or possibly even deserted, she was taken in by Pasteur Vautier and his wife, who at that time had no children of their own. They left Martinique soon after, taking her with them to Le Havre, where the Bucolins were settled. The Vautiers and the Bucolins used to see a good deal of each other. My uncle was at that time employed in a bank abroad, and it was only three years later, when he came home to stay with his people, that he saw little Lucile. He fell in love with her and at once asked her to marry him, to the great grief of his parents and of my mother. Lucile was then sixteen years old. In the meantime Madame Vautier had had two children; she was beginning to be anxious as to the influence their adopted sister – whose character was developing more and more oddly every month – might have over them; the household, moreover, was in straitened circumstances. My mother told me all this in order to explain why the Vautiers accepted her brother's proposal so gladly. What I suppose for my own part is, that Miss Lucile was becoming terribly embarrassing. I am well enough acquainted with Le Havre society to imagine the kind of reception that a girl of such fascinations would meet with. Pasteur Vautier, whom I knew later on, was a gentle creature, at once circumspect and ingenuous, incapable of coping with intrigue and quite defenceless against evil – the worthy man must have been at the end of his tether. I can say nothing of Madame Vautier; she died in giving birth to a fourth child who was about my own age and who afterwards became my friend.

Lucile Bucolin took very little share in our life; she did not come downstairs from her room till after the mid-day meal was over, and then immediately stretched herself on the sofa or in a hammock and remained there till evening, when she would rise, no less languid than before. She used sometimes to raise a handkerchief to her forehead as if wiping away some imaginary moisture, though her skin was a perfection of smooth purity; this handkerchief of hers filled me with wonder because of its fineness and its scent, which seemed more like the perfume of a fruit than of a flower; sometimes she would draw from her waist a minute mirror with a sliding silver lid, which hung with various other objects from her watch-chain; she would look at herself, wet her finger at her lips and then moisten the corner of her eyes. She used often to hold a book, but it was almost always shut; a tortoise-shell bookmarker was stuck between its pages. If you came near her she did not turn from the contemplation of her dreams to look at you. Often from her careless or tired hand, from the back of the sofa or from a fold of her dress, her handkerchief would drop to the ground, or her book, or a flower, maybe, or the bookmarker. One day when I picked up her book – this is a childish memory I am telling you – I blushed to see it was a book of poetry.

In the evening after dinner Lucile Bucolin did not join our family party at the table, but sat down to the piano, where she took a kind of placid pleasure in playing one or other of Chopin's slow mazurkas; sometimes she would break off in the middle of a bar and pause, suspended motionless on a chord.

I used to experience a peculiar discomfort when I was with my aunt: it was a feeling of uneasiness, of disturbance, mingled with a kind of admiration and a kind of terror. Perhaps some obscure instinct set me against her; and then I felt that she despised Flora Ashburton and my mother, and that Miss Ashburton was afraid of her, and that my mother disliked her.

Lucile Bucolin, I wish I no longer bore you malice; I wish I could forget for a moment how much harm you did . . . at any rate, I will try to speak of you without anger.

One day of that summer – or perhaps of the following, for as the place where the scene was laid never changed, my memories sometimes overlap and become confused – one day I went into the drawing-room to fetch a book; she was there. I was on the point of going away again when she called me back – she, who as a rule never seemed to see me.

'Why do you run away so fast, Jerome? Are you afraid of me?'

With a beating heart I drew near, forced myself to smile, put out my hand. She took my hand with one of hers and with the other stroked my cheek. 'How badly your mother dresses you, you poor little thing!' she said.

At that time I used to wear a sort of sailor suit with a large collar, which my aunt began pulling about.

'Sailor collars are worn much more open,' said she, undoing a button of my shirt. 'There, see if that doesn't look better!' and taking out her little mirror, she drew my face down to hers, passed her bare arm around my neck, put her hand into my shirt, asked me laughingly if I was ticklish – went on – further. ... I started so violently that my shirt tore across and with a flaming face I fled, as she called after me:

'Oh, the little stupid!'

I rushed away to the other end of the kitchen-garden, and there I dipped my handkerchief into a little tank, put it to my forehead – washed, scrubbed – my cheeks, my neck, every part of me the woman had touched.

There were certain days on which Lucile Bucolin had one of her 'attacks'. They would come on suddenly and the whole house was turned upside down. Miss Ashburton made haste to get the children out of the way and distract their attention; but it was impossible to stifle or to prevent their hearing the dreadful screams which came from the bedroom or the drawing-room. My uncle lost his head; we heard him rushing along the passages, fetching towels and eau de Cologne and ether; in the evening at table, where my aunt was not yet able to appear, he looked anxious and aged.

When the attack was more or less over, Lucile Bucolin used to send for her children – that is for Robert and Juliette – never for Alissa. On those melancholy days Alissa would shut herself up in her room where her father sometimes joined her, for he used often to talk to Alissa.

My aunt's attacks made a great impression upon the servants. One evening when the attack had been particularly acute and I was being kept in my mother's room, where what was going on in the drawing-room was less noticeable, we heard the cook running along the passages calling out: 'Sir, sir, come quick! My poor lady is dying.'

My uncle had gone up to Alissa's room; my mother went out to meet him on his way down. A quarter of an hour later I heard them talking below the windows of the room where I had remained, and my mother's voice reached me.

'Do you know what I think, my dear? The whole thing is play-acting.' And she repeated the word several times over, emphasizing every syllable, '*play-acting*'.

This was towards the end of the holidays and two years after our bereavement. I was not to see my aunt much oftener. The unhappy event which shattered our family life was preceded by a little incident which occurred a short time before the final catastrophe and turned the uncertain and complex feeling I had hitherto experienced for Lucile Bucolin into pure hatred. But before relating this I must first speak of my cousin.

That Alissa Bucolin was pretty, I was incapable yet of perceiving; I was drawn and held to her by a charm other than mere beauty. No doubt she was very like her mother; but the expression of her eyes was so different that it was not till later that I became aware of this likeness. I cannot describe faces; the features escape me and even the colour of the eyes; I can only recall the expression of her smile – a smile that was already almost sad – and the line of her eyebrows, which were so extra-ordinarily far from her eyes, raised above the eye in a great circle. I have never seen any like them anywhere ... stay, though! there is a Florentine statuette of the time of Dante; and I like to fancy that Beatrice as a child had eyebrows wide-arched like her. They gave her look, her whole being, an expression of inquiry which was at once anxious and confident – yes, of passionate inquiry. She was all question and expectation. You shall hear how this questioning took possession of me, became my life.

And yet Juliette might have been considered more beautiful; the brilliancy of joy and health was upon her; but this beauty of hers beside her sister's grace seemed something external, something which lay open to the whole world at the first glance. As for Robert, there was nothing particular to distinguish him. He was merely a boy of about my own age; I used to play with him and Juliette; with Alissa I used to talk. She mixed very little in our games; as far back as I can remember, I see her serious, gently smiling, reflective. What did we talk about? What can two children talk about? I will try to tell you in a moment, but let me first finish what I have to say about my aunt, so as to have done with her.

Two years after my father's death, my mother and I spent the Easter holidays at Le Havre. We did not stay with the Bucolins, who had comparatively little room in their town house, but with an elder sister of my mother's, whose house was larger. Aunt Plantier, whom I rarely had the opportunity of seeing, had long since been left a widow; I hardly knew her children, who were much older than I was and very unlike me.

The Plantiers' house was not actually in the town, but half way up the small hill called the 'Côte', which overlooks it. The Bucolins lived in the business quarter; a steep short cut led in a few minutes from one house to the other. I used to run up and down it several times a day.

On that particular day I had had lunch at my uncle's. After the meal was over he went out, and I accompanied him as far as his office and then returned home to the Plantiers' to fetch my mother. There I heard that she had gone out with my aunt and would not be back till dinner time. I immediately went down again to the town where I was very rarely free to go by myself, and found my way to the port, which was dreary that day with a sea-fog; I loitered on the quays for an hour or so, and then suddenly I was seized with the desire to go back and take Alissa by surprise, though indeed I had only just left her. I ran back through the town and rang at the Bucolins' door. I was just darting upstairs when the maid who had let me in stopped me.

'Don't go up, Master Jerome. Don't go up! Mistress is having an attack.'

But I brushed past her. It was not my aunt I had come to see. . . . Alissa's room was on the third floor. On the first there was the drawing-room and the dining-room; on the second, my aunt's room, from which voices were coming. The door past which I had to go was open and a flood of light came from the room and fell on the landing: afraid of being seen, I hesitated a moment and drew back into the dark; this is what I beheld to my unspeakable amazement: my aunt was lying on a sofa in the middle of the room; the curtains were drawn, and it was illuminated by the cheerful light of two candelabra full of candles; Robert and Juliette were at her feet and behind her was a strange young man in a lieutenant's uniform. The presence of the two children seems to me today monstrous; at that time in my innocence I thought it reassuring rather than otherwise. They were laughing and looking at the stranger, who was saying in a piping voice:

'Bucolin! Bucolin! . . . If I had a pet lamb I should certainly call it Bucolin.'

My aunt herself burst out laughing. I saw her hold out a cigarette for the young man to light, smoke a few whiffs of it and then let it fall to the floor. He rushed forward to pick it up, made as if he had caught his feet in a scarf, tripped and fell on his knees before my aunt. Thanks to this ridiculous performance, I was able to slip by without being noticed.

I found myself outside Alissa's door. For a moment I waited. Bursts of laughter and voices came up from the floor below; perhaps they drowned the sound of my knock, for I heard no answer. I pushed the door and it opened silently. The room was so dark that I did not at once distinguish Alissa: she was on her knees by the bedside; through the window behind her came the last glimmer of expiring daylight. She turned as I came near, but without getting up, and murmured:

'Oh, Jerome, why have you come back?'

I bent down to kiss her face; her face was bathed in tears. . . .

My whole life was decided by that moment: even to this day I cannot recall it without a pang of anguish. Doubtless I understood very imperfectly the cause of Alissa's wretchedness, but I felt intensely that that wretchedness was far too strong for her little quivering soul, for her fragile body, shaken with sobs.

I remained standing beside her, while she remained on her knees. I could express nothing of the unfamiliar transport of my breast, but I pressed her head against my heart, and I pressed my lips to her forehead, while my whole soul came flooding through them. Drunken with love, with pity, with an indistinguishable mixture of enthusiasm, of self-sacrifice, of virtue, I appealed to God with all my strength – I offered myself up to Him, unable to conceive that existence could have any other object than to shelter this child from fear, from evil, from life. I knelt down at last, my whole being full of prayer. I gathered her to me; vaguely I heard her say:

'Jerome! They didn't see you, did they? Oh! go away quickly. They mustn't see you.'

Then, lower still:

'Jerome, don't tell anyone. Poor papa doesn't know about it. . . .'

I told my mother nothing therefore; but the interminable whisperings that went on between her and Aunt Plantier, the mysterious, preoccupied, distressed looks of the two women, the 'Run along, my dear!' with which they would get rid of me whenever I came within earshot of their confabulations, all went to show that they were not wholly unsuspicious of the Bucolin family secret.

We had no sooner returned to Paris than a telegram recalled my mother to Le Havre. My aunt had run away.

'With anyone?' I asked Miss Ashburton, with whom my mother had left me.

'My dear, you must ask your mother. I can't tell you any-thing,' said our dear old friend, whom this event had filled with consternation.

Two days later she and I set out to rejoin my mother. It was a Saturday. I should see my cousins the next day at church, and that was the one idea that filled my mind; for in my childish thoughts I attached great importance to this sanctification of our meeting. After all, I cared very little for my aunt and made it a point of honour not to question my mother.

There were not many people that morning in the little chapel. Pasteur Vautier, no doubt intentionally, had chosen as his text Christ's words: '*Strive to enter in at the strait gate.*'

Alissa was sitting a few seats in front of me. I saw her face in profile; I gazed at her so intently and with such self-oblivion that it seemed as though it were through her that I heard the words I listened to with such passionate eagerness. My uncle was sitting beside my mother, crying.

The pastor first read the whole text: '*Enter ye in at the strait gate: for wide is the gate and broad is the way that leadeth to destruc-tion, and many there be which go in thereat. Because strait is the gate, and narrow is the way, which leadeth unto life, and few there be that find it.*'

Then, under the different headings of his subject he spoke first of the broad way.... With a mind rapt and as in a dream, I saw my aunt's room: I saw her lying on the sofa, laughing; I saw the brilliant officer, laughing too ... and the very idea of laughter and of joy became an offence and an outrage, became, as it were, the hateful exaggeration of sin!

'*And many there be which go in thereat,*' went on the pastor; then he painted, and I saw, a gaily dressed, laughing multitude, advancing in joyous troops, whom I felt I could not and would not join, because every step I took with them would lead me farther and farther from Alissa. Then the pastor took up again the first words of his text, and I saw that strait gate through which we must strive to enter. I fancied it, in the dream in which I was plunged, as a sort of press into which I passed with effort and with an extremity of pain, that yet had in it as well, a fore-taste of heavenly felicity. And again this gate became the door of Alissa's room; in order to enter in at it, I squeezed myself – I emptied myself of all that I contained of selfishness. . . . *'Because strait is the gate which leadeth unto life,'* went on Pasteur Vautier; and beyond all maceration, beyond all sorrow, I imagined – I had the presentiment of another joy, pure, seraphic, mystic, for which my soul was already athirst. I imagined this joy like the song of a violin, at once strident and tender, like the pointed fierceness of a flame, in which Alissa's heart and mine were consumed. We advanced together, clothed in those white robes of which the Apocalypse speaks, holding each other by the hand, looking forward to the same goal. . . . What if these childish dreams should call up a smile? I repeat them as they came, without alteration. Their apparent confusion lies only in the use of words and imperfect images, to convey a feeling that was perfectly definite.

'*And few there be that find it,*' ended the pastor. He explained how to find the strait gate. . . . '*Few there be –*' I would be one of those. . . .

At the end of the sermon I had reached such a pitch of moral tension that, without attempting to see my cousin, as soon as the service was over, I fled – out of pride, already desiring to put my resolutions (for I had made resolutions) to the test, and thinking that I should so best deserve her.

2

THIS austere teaching found my soul ready prepared and naturally predisposed to duty. My father's and mother's example, added to the puritanical discipline to which they had submitted the earliest impulses of my heart, inclined me still more towards what I used to hear called 'virtue'. Self-control was as natural to me as self-indulgence to others, and this severity to which I was subjected, far from being irksome to me, was soothing. It was not so much happiness which I sought in the future, as the infinite effort to attain it, and in my mind I already confounded happiness with virtue. No doubt, like all boys of fourteen, I was still unformed and pliable, but my love for Alissa soon urged me further and more deliberately along the road on which I had started. A sudden inward illumination made me acquainted with myself. I saw myself as a brooding, half-fledged, wistful creature, somewhat careless of others, somewhat unenterprising, and with no ambitions save for such victories as are to be gained over self. I was fond of my books and cared only for the games which need reflection or effort. I did not much frequent the society of my school-fellows, and when I did take part in their amusements, it was only out of affection or good nature. I made friends, however, with Abel Vautier who, the following year, joined me in Paris and was in my form at school. He was an agreeable, indolent boy, for whom I had more liking than esteem, but at any rate he was someone with whom I could talk about Fongueusemare and Le Havre, where my thoughts were continually flying.

As for my cousin Robert Bucolin, who had been sent to the same school, he was two forms below us and I saw him only on Sundays. If he had not been the brother of my cousins, whom, however, he was very unlike, I should have taken no pleasure in his society.

I was at that time entirely engrossed by my love, and it was in its light alone that these two friendships had any importance for me. Alissa was the Pearl of Great Price of which the Gospel spoke, and I was like him who went and sold all that he had to buy it. Child as I still was, am I wrong in talking of love, and in giving this name to the feeling I had for my cousin? Nothing that I experienced later seems to me worthier of that name – and moreover, when I became old enough to suffer from the more definite qualms of the flesh, my feeling did not greatly change in character; I never sought more directly to possess her whom, as a child, I had sought only to deserve. Work, efforts, pious acts, I offered them all up, mystically, to Alissa, and, indeed, invented a refinement of virtue by which I often left her in ignorance of what I had done only for her sake. In this way I became intoxicated, as it were, with the fumes of modesty, and accustomed myself, alas! regardless of my own comfort, to feel no satisfaction in anything that did not cost me an effort.

Was I alone to feel the spur of emulation? I do not think that Alissa was touched by it, or that she did anything for my sake or for me, though all my efforts were only for her. Everything in her unaffected and artless soul was of the most natural beauty. Her virtue seemed like relaxation, so much there was in it of ease and grace. The gravity of her look was made charming by her childlike smile; I recall that gently and tenderly inquiring look, as she raised her eyes, and can understand how my uncle, in his distress, sought support and counsel and comfort from his elder daughter. In the summer that followed I often saw him talking to her. His grief had greatly aged him; he spoke little at meals, or sometimes displayed a kind of forced gaiety which was more painful than his silence. He remained smoking in his study until the hour of the evening when Alissa would go to fetch him. He had to be persuaded to go out; she led him off to the garden like a child. Together they would go down the flower-walk towards the place at the head of the steps leading down to the kitchen-garden, where we had put out a few chairs.

One evening, I was lingering out of doors reading, and as I lay on the grass in the shade of one of the big copper beeches, separated from the flower-walk only by the laurel hedge, which prevented me from being seen but not from hearing, Alissa's and my uncle's voices reached me. They had no doubt been talking of Robert; then I heard my name uttered by Alissa, and I was just beginning to make out their words, when my uncle exclaimed:

'He! Oh, he will always be fond of work.'

An involuntary listener, my first impulse was to go away, or at any rate make some movement to show them that I was there; but what was I to do? Cough? Call out 'I am here; I can hear you'? It was much more awkwardness and shyness than curiosity to hear more which kept me quiet. And besides, they were only passing by and I heard what they said only very indistinctly. But they came on slowly; Alissa no doubt, as was her habit, with a light basket on her arm, was cutting off the heads of faded flowers and picking up from under the espaliers the unripe fruit, which the frequent sea-mists used so often to bring down. I heard her clear voice:

'Papa, was Uncle Palissier a remarkable man?'

My uncle's voice was low and indistinct: I could not make out his answer. Alissa insisted: 'Very remarkable, do you think?'

Again an inaudible answer and again Alissa's voice:

'Jerome is clever, isn't he?'

How could I help straining to hear? But no! I could make out nothing. She went on:

'Do you think he will become a remarkable man?'

Here my uncle raised his voice:

'First, my dear, I should like to understand what you mean by "remarkable". One can be very remarkable without its showing – at any rate in the eyes of men – very remarkable in the eyes of God.'

'Yes, that is what I mean,' said Alissa.

'And then, one can't tell yet. He's too young. Yes, certainly, he's very promising, but that's not enough for success.'

'What more must there be?'

'Oh, my child! I can hardly tell. There must be confidence, support, love –'

'What do you mean by support?' interrupted Alissa.

'The affection and esteem that have been lacking to me,' answered my uncle, sadly; and then their voices finally died away.

When I said my prayers that evening, I felt remorse for my unintentional eavesdropping and resolved to confess it to my cousin. Perhaps this time there *was* a mixture of curiosity in my resolution.

At my first words the next day, she said:

'But, Jerome, it's very wrong to listen like that. You ought to have told us you were there or else to have gone away.'

'Really, I didn't listen – I just overheard you without meaning to. And you were only passing by.'

'We were walking slowly.'

'Yes, but I hardly heard anything. I stopped hearing almost at once. What did uncle answer when you asked him what was necessary for success?'

'Jerome,' she said, laughing, 'you heard perfectly well. You are just making me repeat it for your amusement.'

'I really heard only the beginning – when he spoke of confidence and love.'

'He said, afterwards, that a great many other things were necessary.'

'And you, what did you answer?'

She suddenly became very serious.

'When he spoke of support in life, I answered that you had your mother.'

'Oh, Alissa, you know I shan't always have her – And then, it's not the same thing –'

She bent her head:

'That's what he said too.'

I took her hand, trembling.

'Whatever I hope to become later is for you.'

'But Jerome, I may leave you too.'

My soul went into my words:

'*I* shall never leave *you*.'

She raised her shoulders slightly:

'Aren't you strong enough to walk alone? We must each of us find God by ourselves.'

'But you must show me the way.'

'Why do you want any other guide but Christ? Do you think we are ever nearer to each other than when each of us forgets the other, as we pray to God?'

'Yes,' I interrupted, 'that He may unite us. That is what I ask Him morning and evening.'

'Don't you understand what communion in God means?'

'With my whole heart I understand. It means being rapturously united in the worship of the same thing. I think it is just because I want to be united to you, that I worship what I know you worship too.'

'Then your worship is not pure.'

'Don't ask too much of me. I shouldn't care for Heaven if you were not there too.'

She put her fingers on her lips and answered with some solemnity:

' "*Seek ye first the kingdom of God and His righteousness.*" '

As I put down our words I feel that they will seem very unchildlike to those who do not realize the deliberate seriousness with which some children talk to each other. What am I to do? Try to excuse them? No! no more than I will colour them to make them look more natural.

We had procured the Gospels in the Vulgate and knew long passages of them by heart. Alissa had learnt Latin with me, under the plea of helping her brother, but really, I think, in order to follow me in my reading. And indeed, I could hardly bring myself to take pleasure in any study in which I knew she would not keep me company. If this was sometimes a hindrance to me, it was not, as might be supposed, because it hampered the growth of my mind; on the contrary, it was she who seemed to be everywhere and easily ahead of me. But the course my mind pursued was always shaped with reference to her, and what preoccupied us at that time, what we called 'thought', was often merely the pretext for some more subtle communion, merely the disguise of feeling, merely the covering of love.

My mother may at first, perhaps, have been anxious about a feeling whose depth she had not as yet gauged. But now that she felt her strength ebbing, she loved to gather us together in the same maternal embrace. The heart disease from which she had long been suffering began to be more and more troublesome. In the course of a particularly severe attack she sent for me:

'My poor boy,' she said, 'I'm getting very old. Some day I shall leave you suddenly.'

She stopped; her breathing was very difficult. Then I broke out, irresistibly, with what it seemed to me she was expecting me to say:

'Mamma . . . you know I want to marry Alissa.' And my sentence was no doubt the continuation of her secret thoughts, for she went on at once:

'Yes, that is what I want to speak to you about, my Jerome.'

'Mamma,' said I, sobbing, 'you do think she loves me, don't you?'

'Yes, my child.' And several times she repeated tenderly: 'Yes, my child.' She spoke with difficulty. She added: 'You must leave it to the Lord.' Then as I was stooping over her, she put her hand on my head and said:

'May God keep you, my children! May God keep you both!' Then she fell into a doze, from which I did not try to rouse her.

27

This conversation was never resumed. The next morning my mother felt better. I went back to school and silence closed again over this semi-confidence. In any case, what more could I have learnt? That Alissa loved me I could not for a moment doubt. And, even if I could, doubt would for ever have vanished from my heart at the time of the melancholy event which occurred soon after.

My mother passed away very quietly one evening when Miss Ashburton and I were with her. The final attack which carried her off had not at first seemed worse than the preceding ones; it was only towards the end that it became alarming and we had no time to send for any of our relations. It was with our old friend that I watched the first night beside my dear mother's body. I loved my mother deeply, and wondered that in spite of my tears I should feel so little sadness. If I wept it was out of pity for Miss Ashburton, whose friend – so many years younger than herself – had thus been taken by God before her. But the secret thought that this bereavement would hasten an understanding with my cousin greatly predominated over my grief.

My uncle arrived the next morning. He handed me a letter from his daughter, who did not come till the day after with Aunt Plantier.

'. . . Jerome, my friend, my brother' [she wrote], '. . . how grieved I am not to have been able to speak those few words to her before her death, which would have given her that great happiness she desired. May she forgive me now! And may God alone guide us both henceforward! Good-bye, my poor friend.

'I am, more tenderly than ever,

'YOUR ALISSA.'

What could be the meaning of this letter? What were those words that she was grieved not to have uttered – what could they be but those with which she would have plighted our future? I was still so young, however, that I dared not ask her for her hand at once. And besides, what need had I of her promise? Were we not already as good as engaged? Our love was no secret from our relations; my uncle was no more opposed to it than my mother had been; on the contrary, he treated me already as a son.

I spent the Easter holidays, which began a few days later, at Le Havre, sleeping at Aunt Plantier's and taking nearly all my meals at Uncle Bucolin's.

My aunt Félicie Plantier was the best of women, but neither my cousins nor I were on very intimate terms with her. She was in a continual state of breathless bustle; her gestures were ungentle and her voice unmusical; she harried us with caresses and at odd moments of the day, when the need for effusion seized her, she would suddenly overwhelm us with the floods of her affection. Uncle Bucolin was very fond of her, but merely from the tone of his voice when he spoke to her, it was easy to understand how greatly he had preferred my mother.

'My poor boy,' she began one evening, 'I don't know what you are meaning to do this summer, but I will wait to hear your plans before settling my own: if I can be useful to you –'

'I have not thought much about it yet,' I answered. 'Perhaps I shall travel.'

She went on:

'You know that both here and at Fongueusemare you will always be welcome. You will be doing your uncle and Juliette a pleasure by going to them . . .'

'Alissa, you mean.'

'Of course. I beg your pardon. . . . Would you believe it? I thought it was Juliette you were in love with! Until a month ago – when your uncle told me – you know I'm very fond of you all, but I don't know you very well; I've seen so little of you. . . . And then I'm not very observant; I have no time to mind other people's business. I always saw you playing with Juliette – I thought to myself, she's so pretty, so gay –'

'Yes, I like playing with her still, but it's Alissa I love.'

'All right, all right! It's your affair. As for me, I hardly know her at all, so to speak. She talks less than her sister. I suppose as you've chosen her you must have good reasons for it.'

'But, Aunt, I didn't choose to love her, and I've never thought what reasons I had for –'

'Don't be cross, Jerome. I didn't mean anything. Now, you've made me forget what I wanted to say. Oh, yes! I suppose, of course, it'll all end with your marrying; but it wouldn't be quite proper for you to become engaged just yet because of your mourning – and then you're still very young. I thought, now that your mother isn't there, your staying at Fongueusemare mightn't be considered quite the thing.'

'But, Aunt, that's just why I spoke of travelling.'

'Oh, well, my dear, I thought that my presence there might make things easier and I've arranged to keep part of the summer free.'

'If I asked Miss Ashburton she would certainly come with pleasure.'

'Yes, I know she's coming already. But that's not enough! I will come too. Oh! I don't pretend I shall take your poor mother's place,' she added, suddenly bursting into sobs, 'but I can look after the housekeeping – and – well – you and your uncle and Alissa needn't feel uncomfortable.'

Aunt Félicie was mistaken as to the efficacy of her presence. To tell the truth we were only uncomfortable because of her. In accordance with her announcement, she settled herself at Fongueusemare at the beginning of July, and Miss Ashburton and I joined her there soon after.

Under the pretence of helping Alissa to look after it, she filled the house, which had always been so peaceful, with a continual hubbub. The zeal with which she set about being agreeable to us and 'making things easier', as she called it, was so overdone that Alissa and I were nearly always constrained

and practically speechless when she was by. She must have
thought us very cold. . . . And even if we had not been silent,
would she have been able to understand the nature of our love?
Juliette's character, on the other hand, fitted in well enough
with this exuberance; and perhaps my affection for my aunt
was tinged with a certain resentment at seeing her show such
a marked preference for the younger of her nieces.

One morning, after the arrival of the post, she sent for me:
'My poor Jerome,' she said, 'I'm absolutely heartbroken;
my daughter is ill and wants me; I shall be obliged to leave
you. . . .'

Puffed up with idle scruples, I went to find my uncle, not
knowing whether I should dare to stay on at Fongueusemare
after my aunt's departure. But at my first words:

'What,' he cried, 'will my poor sister think of next to com-
plicate what is so very natural? Why should you leave us,
Jerome? Aren't you already almost my child?'

My aunt had barely stayed a fortnight at Fongueusemare.
As soon as she was gone the house was able to sink back again
into peace. There dwelt in it once more a serenity that was
very like happiness. My mourning had not cast a shadow on
our love, but had made it weightier. And in the monotonous
course of the life which then began, as if in some place of high
resonance, each slightest stirring of our hearts was audible.

Some days after my aunt's departure I remember we were
discussing her one evening at table:

'What a commotion!' said we. 'It is possible that the stir
of life should leave her soul so little respite? Fair image of
love, what becomes of your reflection here?' . . . For we remembered Goethe's saying about Madame de Stein: 'It would be
beautiful to see the world reflected in that soul.' And we then
and there established a kind of hierarchy, putting the contem-
plative faculties in the highest place. My uncle, who up to then
had been silent, reproved us, smiling sadly:

'My children,' said he, 'God will recognize His image even though broken. Let us beware of judging men from a single moment of their lives. Everything which you dislike in my poor sister is the result of circumstances, with which I am too well acquainted to be able to criticize her as severely as you do. There is not a single pleasing quality of youth which may not deteriorate in old age. What you call "commotion" in Félicie, was at first nothing but charming high spirits, spontaneity, impulsiveness, and grace. We were not very different, I assure you, from what you are today. I was rather like you, Jerome – more so, perhaps, than I imagine. Félicie greatly resembled Juliette as she now is – yes, even physically – and I catch a likeness to her by starts,' he added, turning to his daughter, 'in certain sounds of your voice: she had your smile – and that trick, which she soon lost, of sitting sometimes, like you, without doing anything, her elbows in front of her and her forehead pressed against the locked fingers of her hands.'

Miss Ashburton turned towards me and said almost in a whisper:

'It is your mother that Alissa is like.'

The summer that year was splendid. The whole world seemed steeped in azure. Our fervour triumphed over evil – over death; the shades gave way before us. Every morning I was awakened by my joy; I rose at dawn and sprang to meet the coming day. . . . When I dream of that time, it comes back to me all fresh with dew. Juliette, an earlier riser than her sister, whose habit it was to sit up very late at nights, used to come out into the garden with me. She was the messenger between her sister and me; I talked to her interminably of our love, and she never seemed tired of listening. I told her what I dared not tell Alissa, with whom excess of love made me constrained and shy. Alissa seemed to lend herself to this child's play and to be delighted that I should talk so happily to her sister, ignoring or feigning to ignore that in reality we talked only of her.

Oh, lovely shifts of love, of love's very excess, by what hidden ways you led us, from laughter to tears, from the most artless joy to the exactions of virtue!

The summer sped by so pure, so smooth, that of its swift-slipping days scarce anything remains in my memory. Its only events were talks and readings.

'I have had a melancholy dream,' said Alissa to me on one of the last mornings of the holidays. 'I was alive and you were dead. No, I didn't see you die. It was merely – that you were dead. It was horrible; it was so impossible, that I managed to get it granted for you to be simply absent. We were parted and I felt that there was a way of getting to you; I tried to find out how, and I made such an effort to succeed that it woke me up.

'This morning I think I was under the impression of my dream; it seemed as if it were still going on. I felt as if I were still parted from you – going to be parted from you for a long, long time –' and she added very low: 'all my life – and that all our lives we should have to make a great effort...'

'Why?'

'Each of us a great effort to come together again.'

I did not take these words seriously, or perhaps I was afraid to take them seriously. With a beating heart, and in a sudden fit of courage, I said to her, as though protesting:

'Well, as for me, this morning I dreamt that I was going to marry you – so surely, that nothing, nothing would be able to part us, except death.'

'Do you think that death is able to part?' asked she.

'I mean –'

'I think that death, on the contrary, is able to bring together – yes, bring together what has been parted in life.'

The whole of this conversation sank into us so deeply that I can still hear the very intonation of the words we used. And yet I did not realize all their gravity until later.

The summer sped by. Already nearly all the fields lay bare, with their wider spaces more emptied of hope. The evening before – no, two evenings before my departure, I went out with Juliette and we wandered down to the shrubbery at the end of the lower garden.

'What were you repeating yesterday to Alissa?' she asked.

'When do you mean?'

'When you stayed behind us on the quarry bench.'

'Oh! Some verses of Baudelaire's, I think.'

'What were they? Won't you say them to me?'

'"*Bientôt nous plongerons dans les froides ténèbres,*"' I began rather ungraciously; but no sooner had I started than she interrupted me and took up the lines in a changed and trembling voice: '"*Adieu! vive clarté de nos étés trop courts!*"'

'What! you know them?' I cried, extremely astonished. 'I thought you didn't care for poetry. . . .'

'Why? Because you never repeat me any?' said she, laughing, though in rather a forced way. 'Sometimes you seem to think I'm perfectly idiotic.'

'It's quite possible to be very intelligent and not care for poetry. I've never heard you repeat any or ask me to repeat you any.'

'Because that's Alissa's business.' She was silent for a few minutes and then asked abruptly:

'You're going away the day after tomorrow?'

'Yes, I must.'

'What are you going to do this winter?'

'It's my first year at the École Normale.'

'When do you think of marrying Alissa?'

'Not before I've done my military service. And indeed, not before I have a better idea of what I mean to do afterwards.'

'Don't you know yet?'

'I don't want to know yet. Too many things appeal to me. I want to put off for as long as I can having to choose and settle down to only one thing.'

'Is it reluctance to settle down that makes you put off getting engaged too?'

I shrugged my shoulders without answering. She insisted:

'Then, what are you waiting for? Why don't you get engaged at once?'

'Why should we get engaged? Isn't it enough to know that we do and shall belong to each other, without proclaiming it to the world? Since I choose to devote my whole life to her, do you think it would be nobler to bind my love by promises? Not I! Vows seem to me to be an insult to love. I should only want to be engaged if I distrusted her.'

'It isn't Alissa that I distrust –'

We were walking slowly. We had reached that part of the garden where, in former days, I had unintentionally overheard the conversation between Alissa and her father. It suddenly occurred to me that perhaps Alissa, whom I had seen go out into the garden, was sitting at the head of the steps, and that she would be able to overhear us in the same manner; the possibility of making her listen to words which I dared not say to her openly, tempted me; I was amused by the artifice and raising my voice:

'Oh!' I exclaimed with the somewhat stilted vehemence of youth, and too much engrossed by my own words to hear in Juliette's all that she left unsaid: 'Oh, if only we could lean over the soul we love and see as in a mirror the image we cast there! – read in another as in ourselves, better than in ourselves! What tranquillity there would be in our tenderness – what purity in our love!'

I had the conceit to take Juliette's emotion for an effect of my very indifferent flight of eloquence. She suddenly hid her face on my shoulder:

'Jerome! Jerome! I wish I could be sure you would make her

happy! If she were to suffer through you as well, I think I should detest you!'

'Why, Juliette,' I cried, embracing her and raising her head, 'I should detest myself. If you only knew! Why, it's only that I may begin life better with her, that I don't want to settle on my career yet! Why, it is upon her that I hang my whole future. Why, I want none of the things that I might be without her –'

'And what does she say when you speak to her so?'

'I never speak to her so! Never; and that's another reason why we're not engaged yet; there is never any question of marriage between us, nor of what we shall do hereafter. Oh, Juliette! life with her seems to me so lovely that I dare not – do you understand – I dare not speak to her about it.'

'You want happiness to come on her as a surprise.'

'No! that's not it. But I'm frightened – of frightening her. Do you see? I'm afraid that the immense happiness, which I foresee, may frighten her. One day I asked her whether she wanted to travel. She said that she wanted nothing, that it was enough for her to know that foreign countries existed, and that they were beautiful, and that other people were able to go to them –'

'And you, Jerome, do you want to travel?'

'Yes, everywhere! All life seems to me like a long journey – with her, through books and people and countries. Have you ever thought of the meaning of the words "weighing anchor"?'

'Yes, I often think of them,' she murmured. But barely listening to her, and letting her words drop to earth, like poor, hurt birds, I went on:

'To start one night; to wake up in the dazzling brilliancy of morning; to feel oneself together and alone on the uncertain waves –'

'To arrive in a port, which one has seen on the map as a child; where everything is strange – I imagine you on the gangway, leaving the boat with Alissa leaning on your arm.'

'We should hurry off to the post,' added I, laughing, 'to get the letter which Juliette would have written to us –'

'From Fongueusemare, where she would have stayed behind, and which you would remember as – oh, so tiny, and so sad, and so far away –'

Were those her words exactly? I cannot be sure for, I repeat, I was so full of my love that, beside it, I was scarcely aware of any expression but its own.

We were drawing near the steps, and were just going to turn back, when Alissa suddenly appeared from out of the shade. She was so pale that Juliette uttered an exclamation.

'Yes, I don't feel very well,' Alissa stammered hastily. 'The air is rather chilly. I think I had better go in.' And leaving us there and then, she went hurriedly back towards the house.

'She overheard what we were saying,' cried Juliette, as soon as she was a little way off.

'But we didn't say anything which could have vexed her. On the contrary –'

'Oh! Let me alone,' she said, and darted off in pursuit of her sister.

That night I could not sleep. Alissa had come down to dinner, but had retired immediately afterwards, complaining of a headache. What had she heard of our conversation? I anxiously went over in my mind everything we had said. Then I thought that perhaps I had been wrong to walk so close to Juliette and to let my arm slip round her; but it was the habit of childhood, and many a time Alissa had seen us walking so. Ah! blind wretch that I was, groping after my own errors, not to have thought for a moment that Juliette's words, to which I had paid too little attention, and which I remembered so ill, might perhaps have been better understood by Alissa. No matter! Led astray by my anxiety, terrified at the idea that Alissa might distrust me, and imagining no other peril, I resolved, in spite of what I had said to Juliette, and influenced, perhaps, by what she had said to me – I resolved to overcome my scruples and apprehensions and to betrothe myself the following day.

It was the eve of my departure. Her sadness, I thought, might be ascribed to that. She seemed to avoid me. The day passed without my being able to see her alone. The fear of being obliged to leave before speaking to her sent me to her room a little before dinner. She was putting on a coral necklace, and, her arms raised to fasten it, she was bending forward, with her back turned to the door, looking at herself over her shoulder, in a mirror between two lighted candles. It was in the mirror that she first caught sight of me, and she continued to look at me in it for some moments without turning round.

'Why,' said she, 'wasn't the door shut?'

'I knocked, but you didn't answer. Alissa, you know I'm going tomorrow?'

She answered nothing, but laid down the necklace, which she could not succeed in fastening. The word 'engagement' seemed to me too bare, too brutal; I used I know not what periphrasis in its stead. As soon as Alissa understood what I meant, I thought I saw her sway and lean against the mantel-piece for support – but I myself was trembling so much that in my fearfulness I avoided looking at her.

I was near her, and without raising my eyes, I took her hand; she did not free herself, but bending down her face a little and raising my hand a little, she put her lips on it and murmured, as she half leant against me:

'No, Jerome, no; don't, please, let us be engaged.'

My heart was beating so fast, that I think she felt it, and she repeated, more tenderly:

'No, not yet –'

And as I asked her:

'Why?'

'It's I that ought to ask you why,' she said. 'Why change?'

I did not dare speak to her of yesterday's conversation, but no doubt she felt I was thinking of it, and as if in answer to my thought, said, as she looked at me earnestly:

'You are wrong, dear. I do not need so much happiness. Are we not happy enough as we are?'

She tried in vain to smile.

'No, since I have to leave you.'

'Listen, Jerome, I can't speak to you this evening – don't let's spoil our last minutes. No, no, I'm as fond of you as ever; don't be afraid. I'll write to you; I'll explain. I promise I'll write to you – tomorrow – as soon as you have gone. Leave me now! See, I am crying. You must go.'

She pushed me away, tore me gently from her – and that was our good-bye; for that evening I was not able to speak to her again, and the next morning, when it was time for me to leave, she shut herself up in her room. I saw her at her window, waving good-bye to me as she watched my carriage drive off.

3

I HAD hardly seen Abel Vautier that year; he had enlisted without waiting to be called up, whilst I, in the meantime, had been reading for my degree. I was two years younger than Abel, and had put off my military service until after leaving the École Normale, where we were both of us to go for our first term that year.

We met again with pleasure. After leaving the army, he had spent more than a month travelling. I was afraid of finding him changed; but he had merely acquired more confidence without losing any of his charm. We spent the afternoon before the opening day of the term in the Luxembourg gardens; unable to restrain myself from confiding in him, I spoke to him at length about my love for Alissa, which, for that matter, he knew of already. During the last year he had acquired some experience of women, and, in consequence, put on rather a conceited and patronizing manner, which, however, did not offend me. He laughed at me for not having finally managed to clinch the matter, as he expressed it, giving forth as an axiom, that a woman should never be given time to go back on herself. I let him talk, but thought to myself that his excellent arguments were not applicable either to her or to me, and simply showed that he did not understand us.

The day after our arrival I received the following letter:

'My dear Jerome,

'I have been thinking a great deal about your suggestion.' [My suggestion! What a way of speaking of our engagement!] 'I am afraid I am too old for you. Perhaps you don't think so now, because you have had no opportunity yet of seeing anything of other women. But I keep thinking of what I should suffer later on, if after I had given myself to you, I were to find out that you were no longer able to care for me. You will be very indignant, no doubt, as you read this; I think I hear you protesting; it's not that I doubt your love – I simply ask you to wait a little longer until you are rather better acquainted with life.

'Please understand that I am speaking only of you – as for myself, I feel sure that I shall never cease to love you.

'ALISSA.'

Cease to love each other! Could there be any question of such a thing? I was more astonished than grieved, but so greatly disturbed that I hurried off to show the letter to Abel.

'Well, what do you mean to do?' said he, after he had read the letter, shaking his head and screwing up his lips as he did so. I made a despairing gesture. 'At any rate, I hope you aren't going to answer her! If you begin arguing with a woman you're lost. Listen to me: if we were to sleep at Le Havre on Saturday night, we might spend Sunday morning at Fongueusemare, and be back here in time for the lecture on Monday morning. I haven't seen your people since my military service. That's excuse enough; and a very creditable one. If Alissa sees that it's only an excuse, so much the better. I'll look after Juliette whilst you talk to her sister. Try not to play the fool. To tell you the truth, there's something I can't understand in your tale; you can't have told me everything. Never mind! I'll soon get to the bottom of it. Mind you don't let them know we're coming: you must take your cousin by surprise and not give her time to arm herself.'

My heart was beating fast as I pushed open the garden gate. Juliette came running to meet us at once. Alissa, who was busy in the linen room, made no haste to come down. We were talking to my uncle and Miss Ashburton when at last she entered the drawing-room. If our sudden arrival had upset her, at any rate she managed to show no signs of it. I thought of what Abel had said, and that it was precisely with the intention of arming herself against me, that she had been so long before making her appearance. Juliette's extreme animation made her reserve seem colder still. I felt that she disapproved of my return; at any rate she tried to show disapprobation in her manner, and I dared not imagine that behind this disapprobation there might be hidden another and a livelier feeling. Seated at some distance apart from us, in a corner near the window, she seemed absorbed in a piece of embroidery, the stitches of which she was counting below her breath. Abel talked – fortunately! for, as for me, I felt incapable of saying a word, and if it had not been for the tales he told of his year's service and his travels, this meeting would have had a dismal beginning. My uncle himself seemed unusually thoughtful.

Immediately after lunch, Juliette took me aside and drew me into the garden:

'What do you think?' said she, when we were alone, 'I've had an offer of marriage! Aunt Félicie wrote to papa yeterday to tell him she had had a proposal for me from a Nîmes vine-grower; a person who is very satisfactory in every way, she says; he met me out at some parties last spring and fell in love with me.'

'And did this individual make any impression on you?' I questioned with an instinctive feeling of hostility towards the suitor.

'Yes, I think I remember him. A kind of cheery Don Quixote – not cultivated – very ugly – very vulgar – rather ridiculous; Aunt Félicie couldn't keep her countenance before him.'

'Has he any – chance?' I asked, mockingly.

'Oh, Jerome! How can you? A man who's in business! ... If you'd seen him you wouldn't ask.'

'And has my uncle answered?'

'He answered what I did – that I was too young to marry. Unfortunately,' she added, laughing, 'Aunt foresaw that objection: in a postscript she says that Monsieur Édouard Teissières – that's his name – is willing to wait, that he has simply declared himself so soon in order to be put "on the ranks". It's absurd, but what am I to do? All the same, I can't tell him he's too ugly.'

'No, but you can say that you don't want to marry a vine-grower.'

She shrugged her shoulders:

'That's a kind of reason Aunt's mind is incapable of taking in. But let's talk of something else. Has Alissa written to you?'

She spoke with extreme volubility and seemed in great agitation. I handed her Alissa's letter, which she read, blushing deeply. I seemed to discern a note of anger in her voice as she asked me:

'Then what are you going to do?'

'I don't know,' I answered. 'Now that I am here, I feel as if it would have been easier to write, and I blame myself for coming. Can you understand what she means?'

'I understand she wants to leave you free.'

'Free! What do I care for freedom? And can you understand why she writes to me so?'

She answered 'No!' so shortly that, without at all divining the truth, I at least felt persuaded from that moment that Juliette probably knew something about it. Then, abruptly turning back as we came to a bend in the path: 'Let me be now,' she said. 'You haven't come here to talk to me. We have been together a great deal too long.'

She fled off to the house, and a moment later I heard her at the piano.

When I went back to the drawing-room she was talking to Abel, who had joined her there; she went on playing as she talked, though carelessly, and as if she were vaguely improvising. I left them. I went into the garden and wandered about some time, looking for Alissa.

She was at the bottom of the orchard, picking the first chrysanthemums at the foot of a low wall. The smell of the flowers mingled with that of the dead leaves in the beech copse and the air was saturated with autumn. The sun did no more now than just warm the espaliers, but the sky was orientally pure. Her face was framed, hidden nearly, in the depths of a big

Dutch peasant's cap, which Abel had brought back from his travels and which she had at once put on. She did not turn as I drew near, but I saw, by the slight tremor which she could not repress, that she had recognized my step; and I began at once to fortify myself against her reproaches and the severity which I felt her look was going to impose upon me. But when, as I came closer and, as if afraid, began to slacken my pace, she, although still she did not turn but kept her head lowered as a sulky child might do, stretched out to me from behind her back her hand full of flowers, and seemed to beckon me on. And as, on the contrary, at sight of this gesture I came to a standstill in a spirit of playfulness, she turned round at last and took a few steps towards me, raising her face; and I saw that it was all full of smiles. The brightness of her look made everything seem on a sudden simple again and easy, so that without an effort and with an unaltered voice, I began:

'It was your letter that brought me back.'

'I thought so,' said she, and then softening the sharpness of her rebuke by the inflexion of her voice; 'and that is what vexed me. Why didn't you like what I said? It was very simple, though.' (And indeed, sadness and difficulty seemed now nothing but imagination, seemed now to exist only in my mind.) 'We were happy so; I told you we were; why be astonished at my refusing when you ask me to change?'

And indeed I felt happy with her, so perfectly happy, that the one desire of my mind was that it should differ in nothing from hers, and already I wished for nothing beyond her smile, and to walk with her thus, hand in hand, along a sun-warmed, flower-bordered path.

'If you prefer it,' said I gravely, renouncing at one stroke every other hope, and giving myself up to the perfect happiness of the present, '. . . If you prefer it, we will not be engaged. When I got your letter, I did in fact realize that I was happy and that my happiness was going to cease. Oh! give me back the happiness that I had; I can't do without it. I love you well enough

to wait for you all my life, but that you should cease to love me
or that you should doubt my love, that thought, Alissa, is
unbearable to me.'

'Alas! Jerome, I cannot doubt it.'

And her voice, as she said this, was at once calm and sad; but
the smile which illuminated her remained so serenely beautiful
that I was ashamed of my fears and protestations; it seemed to
me then, that from them alone came that touch of sadness
which I felt lurking in her voice. Without any transition, I
began speaking of my plans and of the new life from which I
was expecting to derive so much benefit. The École Normale
was not at that time what it has since become; its somewhat
rigorous discipline, irksome only to young men of an indolent
or refractory disposition, was helpful to those whose minds were
bent on study. I was glad that this almost monastic way of life
should preserve me from the world, which at best attracted me
but little; the knowledge that Alissa feared it for me would have
been enough to make it appear hateful.

Miss Ashburton had kept on the apartment she had shared
with my mother in Paris. As Abel and I knew hardly anyone in
Paris, we should spend some hours of every Sunday with her;
every Sunday I should write to Alissa and keep her informed of
every detail of my life.

We were now sitting on the edge of an open garden frame
through which were sprawling huge stalks of cucumber plants,
the last fruits of which had been gathered. Alissa listened to me,
questioned me. I had never before felt her tenderness more
solicitous, her affection more pressing. Fear, care, the slightest
stir of emotion even, evaporated in her smile, melted away in
this delightful intimacy, like the mist in the perfect blueness of
the sky.

Then when Juliette and Abel came out to join us, we spent
the rest of the day on a bench in the beech copse, reading aloud
Swinburne's *Triumph of Time*, each of us taking a verse by
turns. Evening drew in.

When the time came for us to be going, Alissa kissed me good-bye, and then half playfully, but still with that elder sister air, which was perhaps called for by my thoughtlessness, and which she was fond of assuming, 'Come,' said she, 'promise me you won't be so romantic for the future.'

'Well, are you engaged?' asked Abel, as soon as we were again alone together.

'My dear fellow, there's no question of that now,' I answered, adding at once in a tone that cut short any further questioning, 'and a very good thing too. I have never been happier in my life than I am tonight.'

'Nor I either!' he cried; then, abruptly flinging his arms around me: 'I've got something wonderful to tell you, something extraordinary! Jerome, I'm madly in love with Juliette! I suspected as much as long ago as last year; but I've seen life since then, and I didn't want to tell you anything about it until I'd met your cousins again. Now it's all up with me! It's for life.

J'aime, que dis-je aimer – j'idolâtre Juliette!

I've thought for a long time past that I had a kind of brother-in-law's affection for you.'

Then, laughing and joking, he embraced me again and again, flinging himself about like a child, on the cushions of the railway carriage that was taking us to Paris. I was absolutely astounded by his announcement; and the slight strain of literary affectation which I felt in it jarred on me not a little; but how was it possible to hold out against such vehemence and such rapture?

'Well, what? Have you proposed to her?' I managed to ask between two bursts of excitement.

'No, no, certainly not!' cried he; 'I don't want to skip the most charming part of the story.

Le meilleur moment des amours
N'est pas quand on a dit: je t'aime. . . .

46

Come now, you aren't going to reproach me with that, are you? You – such a past master of slowness yourself!'

'Well, at any rate,' I said, slightly irritated, 'do you think that she . . .?'

'Didn't you notice her embarrassment when she saw me again? And the whole time of our visit, her agitation, and her blushes and her volubility! No! you noticed nothing, of course! Because you're completely taken up with Alissa. And how she questioned me! How she drank in my words! Her intelligence has tremendously developed since last year. I don't know where you got it that she doesn't like reading; you always imagine that Alissa's the only person who can do anything! My dear boy, it's astonishing what she knows. Can you guess what we were amusing ourselves by doing before dinner? Repeating one of Dante's Canzoni! We each of us said a line, and when I went wrong she corrected me. You know, the one that begins:

Amor che nella mente mi ragiona.

You didn't tell me that she had learnt Italian.'

'I didn't know it myself,' said I, rather astonished.

'What? When we began the Canzone, she told me it was you who had shown it to her.'

'She must have heard me read it to her sister one day when she was sitting with us, doing her needlework, as she often does; but I'm blessed if she ever let on that she understood.'

'Really! You and Alissa are amazing with your egoism. You are so much absorbed in your own love, that you can't spare a glance for the admirable flowering of an intelligence and a soul like hers! I don't want to flatter myself, but all the same it was high time that I appeared on the scene. No, no! I'm not angry with you, as you see,' said he, embracing me again. 'Only promise me – not a word of any of this to Alissa. I want to conduct my affairs by myself. Juliette is caught, that's certain, and fast enough for me to venture to leave her till next holidays. I think I shan't even write to her between this and then. But we

47

will spend the Christmas vacations at Le Havre, and then – '
'And then?'

'Well, Alissa will suddenly learn of our engagement. I mean to push it through smartly. And do you know what will happen? Why! I shall get you Alissa's consent by force of our example. You can't pull it off for yourself, but we shall persuade her that we can't get married before you. . . .'

So he went on, drowning me in an inexhaustible flow of words, which did not stop even on the train's arrival in Paris, even on our getting back to the Normale, for though we walked all the way from the station to the school, he insisted, in spite of the lateness of the hour, on accompanying me to my room, where we went on talking till morning.

Abel's enthusiasm made short work of the present and the future. He already saw and described our double wedding; imagined and painted everybody's surprise and joy; became enamoured of the beauty of our story, of our friendship, of the part he was to play in my love affair. Far from being proof against so flattering a warmth, I felt myself pervaded by it, and gently succumbed to the allurement of his fanciful suggestions. Thanks to our love, courage and ambition swelled in us; we were hardly to have left the École Normale when our double marriage (the ceremony to be performed by Pasteur Vautier) would take place and we should all four start on our wedding journey; then we were each to embark on some monumental work, with our wives as collaborators. Abel, for whom the schoolmaster's profession had no attractions, and who thought he was born to be a writer, would rapidly earn the fortune of which he stood in need, by a few successful plays. As for me, more attracted by learning itself than by the thought of any gain that might accrue from it, my plan was to devote myself to the study of religious philosophy, of which I purposed writing the history – but what avails it now to recall so many hopes?

The next day we plunged into our work.

4

THE time till the Christmas holidays was so short that my faith, quickened as it had been by my last conversation with Alissa, never for a moment wavered. As I had resolved, I wrote to her at length every Sunday; during the rest of the week I kept apart from my fellow-students, and frequented hardly anyone but Abel: I lived with the thought of Alissa, and covered my favourite books with notes meant for her eye, subordinating the interest I sought in them myself to the interest which they might have for her. Her letters caused me some uneasiness; and though she answered mine pretty regularly, her keenness to keep up with me seemed, I thought, to come more from anxiety to encourage my work than from her own spontaneous inclination; and it even seemed to me that, while on my part reflections, discussions, criticisms were only means towards expressing my thoughts, she, on the contrary, took advantage of all these things to conceal hers. Sometimes I wondered whether she were not actually taking pleasure in this as a kind of game. No matter! I was firmly resolved to complain of nothing, and I let no trace of anxiety transpire in my letters.

Towards the end of December, then, Abel and I left for Le Havre.

I was to stay with Aunt Plantier. She was not in when I arrived, but I had hardly time to settle into my room when a servant came to tell me that she was waiting for me in the drawing-room.

She had no sooner finished inquiring after my health, my surroundings, my studies, than, without more ado, she gave way to her affectionate curiosity:

'You haven't told me yet, my dear, whether you were pleased with your stay at Fongueusemare? Were you able to advance matters at all?'

I had to put up with my aunt's good-natured tactlessness, however painful it might be to hear her speak so summarily of feelings for which the purest and gentlest words would still have seemed too brutal; yet her tone was so simple and so cordial that it would have been senseless to take offence. Nevertheless, I could not help objecting a little.

'Didn't you say last spring that you thought an engagement would be premature?'

'Yes, I know; one always says that to begin with,' she started off again, seizing one of my hands, which she pressed with emotion between both of hers. 'Besides, on account of your studies and your military service, you won't be able to marry for several years, I know. Moreover, personally I don't approve of long engagements. They're trying for young girls, though sometimes it's very touching to see ... for that matter it's not necessary to make the engagement public ... only then one can give people to understand – oh! very discreetly – that there's no further need to be on the look-out; and besides, it authorizes your correspondence, your intimacy; and moreover, if anyone else came forward – and it might very well happen,' she insinuated with a knowing smile, 'one is able just to hint that ... no, it's not worth while. You know there's been an offer for Juliette! She has attracted a great deal of attention this winter. She's still rather young, which is what she answered; but the young man suggested waiting; he's not exactly a young man, either ... in short, he's a very good match, a very reliable person. Well! you'll see him tomorrow; he's going to be at my Christmas tree. You'll tell me what you think of him.'

'I'm afraid, Aunt Félicie, that it's labour lost on his part, and that Juliette has someone else in her mind,' said I, making a great effort not to mention Abel straight off.

'Hum?' said Aunt Félicie, inquiringly, and putting her head on one side with an incredulous look. 'You surprise me! Why should she not have told me anything about it?'

I bit my lips to prevent myself from saying anything more.

'Oh, well! we shall soon see. Juliette hasn't been very well lately,' she went on. '. . . but we aren't speaking of her for the moment. Ah! Alissa is very charming too. Come now, did you or did you not make your declaration?'

Although rebelling with my whole heart against the word 'declaration', which seemed to me so inappropriate and crude, I was incapable of replying by a falsehood to this direct question; I answered 'Yes,' in some confusion, and felt my face flame as I did so.

'And what did she say?'

I bent my head: I should have liked not to answer. In still greater confusion and as though in spite of myself, I said, 'She refused to be engaged.'

'Well, the child was quite right,' said my aunt. 'You have plenty of time before you, Heaven knows. . . .'

'Oh! Aunt! that's enough now,' I said, trying in vain to stop her.

'Besides, I'm not surprised; I always thought your cousin more sensible than you. . . .'

I do not know what came over me at this point; my nerves were no doubt exasperated by this cross-examination, for it seemed to me that on a sudden my heart burst; like a child, I buried my face in my kind aunt's lap and cried out, sobbing:

'No, Aunt, no! You don't understand. She didn't ask me to wait –'

'What! Did she refuse you?' said she, in a tone of the kindest commiseration, raising my head with her hand.

'No – no – not exactly.' I shook my head sadly.

'Are you afraid she doesn't love you any longer?'

'Oh, no! I'm not afraid of that.'

'My poor boy, if you want me to understand, you must explain a little more clearly.'

I was ashamed and vexed to have given way to my emotion; my aunt was doubtless incapable of understanding the reasons of my uncertainty; but if some special motive lay behind

Alissa's refusal, Aunt Félicie, by questioning her gently, might perhaps help me to discover it. She soon reached the same conclusion for herself.

'Listen,' she went on, 'Alissa is coming tomorrow morning to help me decorate the Christmas tree; I shall soon see what is at the bottom of it all; I will let you know at lunch time, and I'm sure you'll see there's nothing to be alarmed about.'

I went to dine at the Bucolins'. Juliette, who had, it is true, been unwell for the last few days, seemed to me changed; her eyes had a *farouche*, an almost hard, expression, which made her more different than ever from her sister. I was not able to speak to either of them alone that evening; neither did I wish to, and as my uncle seemed tired I left soon after dinner.

At the Christmas tree which Aunt Plantier gave every year, there was always a large gathering of children, relations, and friends. It was set up in an inner hall, which contained the staircase and out of which opened the entrance hall, the drawing-room, and the glass doors of a kind of winter-garden, where a buffet had been spread. The decoration of the tree was not finished, and on the morning of the party, which was the day after my arrival, Alissa, as my aunt had told me she would, came round pretty early in order to help her hang the branches of the tree with ornaments, lights, fruits, sweets, and toys. I should have very much enjoyed sharing this task with her myself, but I had to let Aunt Félicie speak to her. I went out, therefore, without seeing her, and spent the whole morning in trying to while away the anxious hours.

I first went to the Bucolins', as I wanted to see Juliette. But I heard that Abel had been before me, and as I was afraid of interrupting a crucial conversation, I left at once: then I wandered about the quays and streets till lunch time.

'Great silly!' cried my aunt, when I saw her. 'It's really inexcusable to make yourself so unhappy for nothing! There's not a single word of sense in anything you said to me yesterday. Oh! I didn't beat about the bush. I sent Miss Ashburton away as she was tiring herself out helping us, and as soon as I was alone with Alissa I asked her straight out why she hadn't accepted you last summer. Do you suppose she minded? She wasn't embarrassed for a single moment, and answered quite calmly that she didn't want to marry before her sister. If you had asked her frankly, she would have said the same thing to you; a fine thing to make such a fuss about, isn't it? You see, my dear, there's nothing like frankness. Poor Alissa! She spoke to me about her father, too, whom she can't leave. Oh! we had a long talk. Dear child! She's very sensible; she told me she wasn't perfectly sure yet that she was the right person for you; that she was afraid she was too old, and thought that somebody of Juliette's age . . .'

My aunt went on, but I no longer listened; there was only one thing which mattered – Alissa refused to marry before her sister. But was not Abel there? After all, in his egregious conceit he was right; he was going to pull off, as he said, both our marriages at one blow.

I hid from my aunt, as best I could, the agitation into which this revelation, simple as it was, had plunged me, and showed her nothing but a delight which she thought very natural, and with which she was all the more gratified as it seemed that it was through her that I had obtained it; but directly after luncheon I left her with some excuse or other, and hurried off to find Abel.

'Ah! what did I tell you?' said he, embracing me, as soon as I had confided my good news to him. 'My dear fellow, I can tell you already that the conversation I had with Juliette this morning almost settled it, though we talked of hardly anything but you. But she seemed tired – nervous – I was afraid of agitating her by going too far, of over-exciting her if I stayed too long. But after what you tell me, I hesitate no longer! I snatch up my hat, dear boy, my stick, and I'm off. Come with me as far as the Bucolins' to hang on to my coat-tails, for fear I should fly away on the road; I feel lighter than Euphorion! When Juliette knows that it's only because of her that her sister has refused you – when I make my offer on the spot – Ah! my boy, I can see my father this evening beside the Christmas tree, praising the Lord and weeping with joy, as he extends his hands over the two couples kneeling at his feet; Miss Ashburton will flutter off in a sigh; Aunt Plantier will dissolve into her bodice, and the fiery tree will sing the glory of God and clap its hands, like the mountains in the Scriptures.'

It was towards evening that the Christmas tree was to be lighted, and that the party of children, relations, and friends was to assemble. Not knowing what to do with myself, sick with anxiety and impatience, after I had left Abel I started on a long walk over the cliffs, so as to get over the time of waiting as best I could – lost my way, and altogether managed so cleverly, that when I got back to Aunt Plantier's the party was already in full swing.

As soon as I got into the hall, I caught sight of Alissa; she seemed to be waiting for me, and came towards me at once. She was wearing round her neck, in the opening of her bodice, a little, old, amethyst cross, which I had given her in memory of my mother, but which I had never seen her wear before. Her features were drawn, and the look of suffering on her face smote my heart.

'Why are you so late?' she said rapidly and breathlessly. 'I wanted to speak to you.'

'I lost my way on the cliffs. . . . But you're ill. . . . Oh, Alissa! what is the matter?'

She stood before me a moment, as though she were struck dumb, her lips trembling. So sickening a dread took hold of me that I dared not question her. She put her hand on my neck, as though to pull my face towards her; I saw she wanted to speak, but at that moment some guests came in; disheartened, she let her hand drop. . . .

'It is too late,' she murmured. Then, seeing my eyes fill with tears, she added in reply to my inquiring look – as though such a derisory explanation could suffice to tranquillize me! –

'No . . . don't be alarmed; I've only a headache, the children make such a noise . . . I had to take refuge here . . . it's time to go back to them now.'

She left me abruptly. Some people coming in separated me from her. I thought I should be able to rejoin her in the drawing-room. I caught sight of her at the other end of the room, surrounded by a troop of children whose games she was organizing; between her and me there were a number of people whom I knew, and whom I should not have been able to venture past without running the risk of being stopped. I felt incapable of civilities, of conversation; perhaps if I edged along the wall . . . I tried.

Just as I was going to pass in front of the large glass doors which led into the garden, I felt my arm seized. Juliette was there, half hidden in the embrasure, behind the folds of the curtain.

'Let's go into the conservatory,' she said, hastily. 'I want to speak to you. Go on by yourself; I'll join you there directly.' Then, half opening the door for a moment, she slipped into the garden.

What had happened? I wished I could see Abel. What had he said? What had he done? Returning to the hall, I made my way to the conservatory, where Juliette was waiting for me.

Her face was flaming, her frowning brows gave her look an expression of hardness and pain; her eyes shone as if she were feverish; even her voice was harsh and tense. A sort of fury inspired her; notwithstanding my anxiety I was astonished – embarrassed almost – by her beauty. We were alone.

'Has Alissa spoken to you?' she asked at once.

'Barely two words; I came in very late.'

'You know she wants me to marry before she does?'

'Yes.'

She looked at me fixedly . . .

'And do you know whom she wants me to marry?'

I did not answer.

'You!' she went on with a cry.

'Why! it's madness!'

'Yes! isn't it!' There was both despair and triumph in her voice. She straightened herself, or rather flung herself backwards.

'Now I know what there remains for me to do,' she added indistinctly, as she opened the door of the garden which she slammed violently behind her.

My brain and heart were in a whirl. I felt the blood throbbing in my temples. One sole idea survived in the confusion of my spirits – to find Abel; he, perhaps, would be able to explain the singular behaviour of the two sisters. But I dared not go back to the drawing-room where I thought everyone would see my agitation. I went out. The icy air of the garden calmed me; I stayed in it some time. Evening was falling, and the sea-mist hid the town; there were no leaves on the trees; earth and sky seemed one immense desolation. The sound of voices singing rose upon the air; no doubt it was the choir of children gathered round the Christmas tree. I went in by the entrance hall. The doors of the drawing-room and inner hall were open; in the drawing-room, which was now deserted, I caught sight of my aunt, where she was sitting, partly concealed by the piano, talking to Juliette. In the inner hall the guests were thronging round the lighted tree. The children had finished their hymn; there was a silence, and Pasteur Vautier, standing up in front of the tree, began a sort of sermon. He never missed an opportunity of what he called 'sowing the good seed'. I felt the lights and heat uncomfortably oppressive, and was going out. Abel was standing beside the door; he had, no doubt, been there some time. He was looking at me in a hostile manner, and when our eyes met he shrugged his shoulders. I went towards him.

'Fool!' he said in a whisper; and then, abruptly, 'oh, let's go out; I'm fed up with preaching.'

And as soon as we were outside, 'You fool!' he said again, as I looked at him anxiously, without speaking. 'Why, it's you she loves, you fool! Couldn't you have told me?'

I was aghast. I tried not to understand.

'No, of course not! You couldn't even see it for yourself!' He had seized me by the arm and was shaking me furiously. His voice between his clenched teeth hissed and trembled.

'Abel, I implore you,' I said after a moment's silence, and in a voice which trembled too, while he strode along at random, dragging me with him. 'Instead of being so angry, try to tell me what has happened. I know nothing.'

He stopped suddenly and scrutinized my face by the dim light of a street lamp; then, drawing me quickly to him, he put his head upon my shoulder and murmured with a sob:

'Forgive me! I'm an idiot too, and I didn't understand any better than you, my poor brother!'

His tears seemed to calm him a little; he raised his head, started walking again, and went on:

'What happened? What's the use of going over it again? I had talked to Juliette in the morning, as I told you. She was extraordinarily beautiful and animated; I thought it was because of me, but it was simply because we were talking of you.'

'Didn't you realize it at the time?'

'No, not exactly; but now the smallest detail becomes clear.'

'Are you sure you are not making a mistake?'

'A mistake! My dear fellow, you must be blind not to see that she's in love with you.'

'Then Alissa . . .'

'Then Alissa is sacrificing herself. She had found out her sister's secret, and wanted to give you up to her. Really, old boy, it's not very difficult to understand! I wanted to speak to Juliette again; at my first words, or rather, as soon as she began to understand me, she got up from the sofa where she was sitting and repeated several times over, "I was sure of it," in the tone of voice of a person who was anything but sure.'

'Oh! don't joke about it.'

'Why not? I consider it a highly comic affair. She rushed into her sister's room; I overheard their voices raised excitedly in a way that alarmed me. I hoped to see Juliette again, but after a moment it was Alissa who came out. She had her hat on, seemed embarrassed at seeing me, said "How do you do?" to me quickly as she went out – and that's all.'

'Didn't you see Juliette again?'

Abel hesitated for a little.

'Yes. After Alissa had gone, I pushed open the door of the room. Juliette was there motionless, standing in front of the chimney-piece, her elbows on the marble, her chin in her hands; she was staring at herself in the glass. When she heard me she didn't turn round, but stamped her foot, crying, "Oh, leave me alone!" so harshly that I went away again without asking for more. That's all.'

'And now?'

'Oh! talking to you has done me good. .... And now? Well! you had better try and cure Juliette of her love, for, either I don't know Alissa, or else she won't have you before you do.'

We walked on for some time silently.

'Let's go back,' said he at last. 'The guests must have gone by now. I'm afraid my father will be waiting for me.'

We went in. The drawing-room was, in fact, empty; and in the hall round the tree, whose branches had been stripped and whose lights had been nearly all extinguished, there remained only my aunt and two of her children, Uncle Bucolin, Miss Ashburton, the pastor, my cousins, and a rather ridiculous-looking individual, whom I had noticed talking for a long time to my aunt, but whom I only at that moment recognized as the suitor Juliette had spoken to me about. Taller, stronger, more highly coloured than any of us, almost bald, of a different class, a different world, a different race, he seemed to realize that he was a stranger among us; he wore an immense moustache and a grizzled imperial, which he was nervously twisting and tugging.

The entrance hall, the doors of which had been left open, was not lighted; we had come in noiselessly, and no one noticed our presence. A frightful foreboding shot through me.

'Stop!' said Abel, seizing me by the arm.

Then we saw the stranger draw near Juliette, and take the hand which she abandoned to him without resistance, without giving him a glance. Night shut down upon my heart.

'Oh, Abel! What is happening?' I whispered, as if I did not understand yet, or hoped I did not understand aright.

'By Jove! the young one is going one better,' he said in a hissing voice. 'She doesn't want to be outdone by her sister. The angels are applauding in Heaven, and no mistake!'

My uncle went up to embrace Juliette, whom Miss Ashburton and my aunt were pressing round. Pasteur Vautier drew near. I took a step forward. Alissa caught sight of me, ran up to me in a quiver of emotion.

'Oh, Jerome! It mustn't be. She doesn't love him! Why, she told me so only this very morning! Try to prevent it, Jerome! Oh! what will become of her?'

She hung upon my shoulder with desperate entreaty. I would have given my life to lessen her anguish.

Suddenly there came a cry from near the tree, a confused stir. We rushed up. Juliette had fallen unconscious into my aunt's arms. They were all crowding round, hanging over her, so that I could hardly see her; her face, which had turned frightfully pale, looked as though it were being dragged backwards by the weight of her loosened hair. It seemed, from the convulsive movements of her body, that this was no ordinary faint.

'No, no!' said my aunt aloud, in order to reassure Uncle

Bucolin, who was getting agitated, and whom Pasteur Vautier was already consoling, with his forefinger pointed heavenwards. 'No, it's nothing. The effect of emotion. Just a nervous attack. Monsieur Teissières, please help me, you're so strong. We will carry her up to my room, on to my bed, on to my bed.' Then she stooped towards the elder of her sons, whispered something in his ear, and I saw him go off at once, no doubt to fetch a doctor.

My aunt and the stranger were supporting Juliette's shoulders, as she lay, half reclining, in their arms. Alissa raised her sister's feet and embraced them tenderly. Abel held up her head, which would have fallen backwards, and I saw him bend down and cover with kisses her floating hair, as he gathered it together.

Outside the door of the room I stopped. Juliette was laid on the bed; Alissa said a few words to M. Teissières and to Abel, which I could not hear; she accompanied them to the door and begged us to leave her sister to rest; she wished to remain alone with her, with no one else but Aunt Plantier. Abel caught hold of my arm and dragged me out of doors, into the night, and there we walked on and on for a long time, without purpose, without courage, without reflection.

5

I SEEMED to have no other reason for living than my love, and to that I clung, expecting nothing, and with my mind made up to expect nothing, but what should come to me from Alissa.

The next morning, as I was getting ready to go and see her, my aunt handed me the following letter which she had just received:

'... Juliette's extreme restlessness did not yield to the doctor's prescriptions till towards morning. I beg Jerome not to come and see us for some days. Juliette might recognize his footsteps or his voice, and she is in need of the greatest quiet.

'I am afraid Juliette's condition will keep me here. If I do not manage to see Jerome before he leaves, please tell him, dear Aunt, that I will write to him. ...'

The Bucolins' door was shut only against me. My aunt, or anyone else that chose, was free to knock at it; and, indeed, my aunt was going there that very morning. I might make a noise! What a feeble excuse! No matter.

'Very well,' said I, 'I won't go.'

It cost me a great deal not to see Alissa again at once, and yet I was afraid of seeing her, I was afraid she might hold me responsible for her sister's condition, and it was easier to bear not seeing her again than seeing her vexed.

At any rate, I determined I would see Abel.

At his door, the maid gave me a note:

'I am leaving you this word or two so that you mayn't be anxious. The idea of staying at Le Havre, so near Juliette, was intolerable. I embarked for Southampton last night, almost directly after I left you. I shall spend the rest of the holidays with S— in London. We shall meet again at the School.'

All human help failed me at one and the same time. I did not prolong a stay which could only prove painful to me, and went back to Paris before the beginning of the term. It was to God that I turned my looks, to Him 'from whom cometh down all true consolation and every good gift.' It was to Him that I offered my trouble. I thought that Alissa, too, was taking refuge in Him, and the thought that she was praying encouraged and exalted my prayers.

There went by a long period of meditation and study with no other events but Alissa's letter to me and mine to her. I have kept all her letters; by their help I can, from this time onwards, check my recollections when they become confused.

I had news of Le Havre from my aunt, and at first only from her; I learnt through her what anxiety Juliette's unhappy condition had caused for the first few days. Twelve days after I had left I at last received this letter from Alissa:

'Forgive me, my dear Jerome, for not having written to you sooner. Our poor Juliette's state has allowed me very little time. Since you went away, I have hardly left her. I begged Aunt to give you news of us, and I suppose she has done so. So you know that Juliette had been better for the last three days. I already thank God, but I dare not feel happy yet.'

Robert also, of whom I have so far told you very little, was able to give me news of his sisters, when he returned to Paris a few days after me. For their sake, I spent more time with him than my disposition would have naturally inclined me to; whenever the School of Agriculture, where he was studying, left him free, I took him in charge and was at great pains to amuse him.

It was through him that I learnt – what I had not dared ask either Alissa or my aunt – that Édouard Teissières had come to inquire for Juliette very assiduously, but when Robert had left Le Havre she had not yet seen him. I learnt also that Juliette had kept up an obstinate silence towards her sister, which nothing had been able to break down.

Then I learnt from my aunt a little later that Juliette insisted on her engagement being made public, in spite of what I instinctively felt was Alissa's hope that it would be broken off at once. Advice, injunctions, entreaties, spent themselves in vain against this determination of Juliette's, which seemed fixed like a bar across her brow and like a bandage over her eyes – which seemed to immure her in silence.

Time passed. I received from Alissa – to whom, indeed, I knew not what to write – nothing but the most elusive notes. The thick fogs of winter wrapped me round; my study lamp and all the fervour of my love and faith served but ill, alas! to keep the darkness and the cold from my heart.

Time passed. Then, one morning of sudden spring, came a letter from Alissa to my aunt, who was absent from Le Havre, a letter which my aunt sent on to me and from which I copy out the part that throws light on my story.

'Admire my docility. As you advised, I have seen M. Teissières and talked to him at length. I confess that his behaviour has been perfect, and I have almost, I admit, come to the point of believing that the marriage may not turn out so badly as I feared at first. Certainly Juliette does not love him; but he seems to me every week to be less unworthy of her love. He speaks of the situation with great clear-sightedness and makes no mistake as to my sister's character; but he has great faith in the efficacy of his own love, and flatters himself that there is nothing his constancy will not be able to overcome. That is to say, he is very much in love.

'Yes! I am extremely touched to see Jerome take so much trouble over my brother. I imagine that he does so only out of a sense of duty, for Robert's character is very different from his – perhaps, too, in order to please me – but doubtless he has already come to understand that the more arduous the duty one assumes, the more it educates and uplifts the soul. You will think these very lofty reflections, but do not laugh at your foolish niece too much, for it is these thoughts which give me support and which help me to try and look upon Juliette's marriage as a good thing.

'Dear aunt, your affectionate solicitude is very precious to me. But do not think I am unhappy, I might almost say the contrary is the case, for the trial through which Juliette has just gone has had its effect on me too. Those words of Scripture which I used to repeat without very well understanding them, have suddenly become clear to me: "Cursed be the man that trusteth in man." Long before coming across them in my Bible, I had read them on a little Christmas card which Jerome sent me when he was not quite twelve years old and when I was just fourteen. Beside the bunch of flowers which was painted on it, and which we then thought lovely, there were these lines, from a paraphrase of Corneille's:

> 'Quel charme vainqueur du monde
> Vers Dieu m'élève aujourd'hui?
> Malheureux l'homme qui fonde
> Sur les hommes son appui.

'I confess I infinitely prefer the simple text out of Jeremiah. No doubt, Jerome chose the card at the time without paying much attention to the lines. But if I am to judge from his letters, his frame of mind at present is not unlike mine, and every day I thank God that He should have brought us both nearer to Him with one and the same stroke.

'I have not forgotten our conversation, and I am not writing to him as much as I used to do, so as not to disturb him in his work. You will no doubt think that I make up for it by talking about him all the more; lest I should go on too long, I will end my letter at once. Don't scold me too much this time.'

What reflections this letter aroused in me! I cursed my aunt's meddling interference (what was the conversation to which Alissa alluded, and which was the cause of her silence?) and the clumsy good-nature which made her send the letter on to me. It was already hard enough for me to bear Alissa's silence, and oh! would it not have been better a thousand times to have left me in ignorance that she was writing to another person what she no longer cared to say to me? Everything in the letter irritated me; to hear her speak to my aunt so easily of our little private affairs, as well as the naturalness of her tone, her composure, her seriousness, her pleasantry.

'No, no, my dear fellow! Nothing in the letter irritates you, except the fact that it isn't addressed to you,' said Abel, who was my daily companion; for Abel was the only person to whom I could speak, and in my loneliness I was constantly drawn to him afresh by weakness, by a wistful longing for sympathy, by diffidence, and, when I was at fault, by my belief in his advice, in spite of the difference of our natures – or rather, because of it.

'Let us study this paper,' said he, spreading the letter out on his writing-table.

Three nights had already passed over my vexation; for four days I had managed to keep it to myself! I led up almost naturally to a point when Abel said to me:

'We'll consign the Juliette-Teissières affair to the fire of love – eh? We know what that flame is worth. Upon my word, Teissières seems just the kind of moth to singe his wings in it.'

'That will do!' said I, for his banter was very distasteful to me. 'Let's go on to the rest.'

'The rest,' he said. 'The rest is all for you. You haven't much to complain of. Not a line, not a word, that isn't filled with the thought of you. You may say the whole letter is addressed to you; when Aunt Félicie sent it on to you, she merely sent it to its rightful owner; Alissa writes to the good lady as a make-shift, in default of you. What can Corneille's lines (which, by the way, are by Racine) matter to your aunt? I tell you it's to you she is talking; she's saying it all to you. You're nothing but a simpleton if a fortnight hence your cousin isn't writing to you just as lengthily, as easily, as agreeably . . .'

'She doesn't seem to be taking the right road!'

'It only depends upon you for her to take it! Do you want my advice? Don't say a word for ever so long, of love or marriage; don't you see that since her sister's misfortune, it's *that* she's set against? Harp on the fraternal string and talk to her untiringly of Robert – since you have the patience to look after the young ass. Just go on amusing her intelligence; all the rest will follow. Ah! if it were only I who had to write to her!'

'You aren't worthy to love her.'

Nevertheless, I followed Abel's advice; and, indeed, Alissa's letters soon began to get more animated; but I could not hope for any real joy on her part, or that she would let herself go without reserve, until Juliette's situation, if not her happiness, was assured.

The news which Alissa gave me of her sister improved, however. Her marriage was to take place in July; Alissa wrote to me that she supposed that at this date Abel and I would be engaged in our studies. I understood that she judged it better for us not to appear at the ceremony, so we alleged some examination or other, and contented ourselves with sending our good wishes.

About a fortnight after the marriage this is what Alissa wrote to me:

'My dear Jerome,

'Imagine my astonishment yesterday when, on opening at random the charming Racine you gave me, I found the four lines which are on your little old Christmas card that I had kept in my Bible for the last ten years:

> 'Quel charme vainqueur du monde
> Vers Dieu m'élève aujourd'hui?
> Malheureux l'homme qui fonde
> Sur les hommes son appui!

'I had thought they came from a paraphrase of Corneille's, and I admit I didn't think much of them. But as I went on reading the fourth *Cantique Spirituel*, I came across some verses which are so beautiful, that I cannot resist copying them. No doubt you know them already, if I am to judge from the indiscreet initials which you have put in the margin of the book.' [It is true that I had taken the habit of sprinkling my books and Alissa's with the first letter of her name, opposite all the passages which I liked and which I wanted her to know.] 'Never mind! I write them out for my own pleasure. I was a little vexed at first to see that you had pointed out what I thought was a discovery of my own, but this naughty feeling soon gave way to my pleasure in thinking that you like them as much as I do. As I copy I feel as if I were reading them over with you.

'De la sagesse immortelle
La voix tonne et nous instruit.
Enfants des hommes, dit-elle,
De vos soins quel est le fruit?
Par quelle erreur, âmes vaines,
Du plus pur sang de vos veines
Achetez-vous si souvent,
Non un pain qui vous repaisse,
Mais une ombre qui vous laisse
Plus affamés que devant?

'Le pain que je vous propose
Sert aux anges d'aliment:
Dieu lui-même le compose.
De la fleur de son froment.
C'est ce pain si délectable
Que ne sert point à sa table
Le monde que vous suivez.
Je l'offre à qui veut me suivre.
Approchez. Voulez-vous vivre?
Prenez, mangez et vivez.

*

'L'âme heureusement captive
Sous ton joug trouve la paix,
Et s'abreuve d'une eau vive
Qui ne s'épuise jamais.
Chacun peut boire en cette onde:
Elle invite tout le monde;
Mais nous courons follement
Chercher des sources bourbeuses
Ou des citernes trompeuses
D'où l'eau fuit à tout moment.

'How beautiful! Jerome, how beautiful! Do you really think it as beautiful as I do? A little note in my edition says that Mme de Maintenon, when she heard Mlle d'Aumale sing this hymn, seemed struck with admiration, "dropped a few tears", and made her repeat a part of the piece over again. I know it by heart now, and never weary of saying it to myself. My only regret is that I haven't heard you read it.

'The news from our travellers continues to be very good. You know already how much Juliette enjoyed Bayonne and Biarritz in spite of the fearful heat. Since then they have visited Fontarrabia, stayed at Burgos and crossed the Pyrenees twice. Now she writes me an enthusiastic letter from Montserrat. They think of spending ten days longer at Barcelona before they return to Nîmes, where Édouard wants to be back before September, so as to be able to look after the vintage.

'Father and I have been settled at Fongueusemare for a week now, and we expect Miss Ashburton and Robert in four days' time. You know the poor boy has failed in his examination; not that it was difficult, but the examiner asked him such peculiar questions that it confused him; I cannot believe, after what you told me about his keenness for work, that he hadn't prepared properly, but this examiner, it appears, takes a pleasure in putting people out.

'As for your successes, my dear, I can hardly say that I congratulate you. I have so much confidence in you, Jerome! Whenever I think of you, my heart fills with hope. Will you be able to begin the work you speak about at once?

'Nothing is changed here in the garden; but the house seems very empty! You will have understood – won't you? – why I asked you not to come this year. I feel it is better so; I tell myself so every day, for it is hard to stay so long without seeing you. Sometimes I look for you involuntarily; I stop in the middle of what I am reading, I turn my head quickly . . . it seems as though you were there!

'I continue my letter. It is night, everybody is asleep; I am sitting up late writing to you, before the open window. The garden is full of scents; the air is warm. Do you remember when we were children, whenever we saw or heard anything very beautiful, we used to say to ourselves, "Thanks, Lord, for having created it." Tonight I said to myself with my whole soul, "Thanks, Lord, for having made the night so beautiful!" And suddenly I wanted you there – I felt you there, close to me – with such violence that perhaps you felt it.

'Yes, you were right in your letter when you said, "In generous hearts admiration is lost in gratitude." How many other things I should like to write to you! I think of the radiant land Juliette speaks of. I think of other lands, vaster, more radiant still, more desert-like. A *strange* conviction dwells in me that one day – but I cannot tell how – you and I will see together some great mysterious land – but ah! I cannot tell which . . .'

No doubt you can easily imagine with what transports of joy I read this letter, with what sobs of love! Other letters followed. Alissa, it is true, thanked me for not coming to Fongueusemare; it is true she begged me not to try and see her again this year, but she regretted my absence, she wanted me; from page to page there sounded the same appeal. Where did I find strength to resist it? In Abel's advice, no doubt, and in the fear of suddenly ruining my joy, and in an instinctive stiffening of my will against the inclinations of my heart.

From the letters which followed I copy all that bears upon my tale:

'Dear Jerome,

'My heart melts with joy as I read you. I was just going to answer your letter from Orvieto, when the one from Perugia and the one from Assisi arrived together. My mind has turned traveller; it is only my body that makes believe to stay behind here; in truth I am with you on the white roads of Umbria. I set out with you in the morning and watch the dawn with a fresh-created eye. . . . Did you really call me on the terrace of Cortona? I heard you. We were terribly thirsty on the hills above Assisi, but how good I thought the Franciscan's glass of water! Oh, my friend! It is through you that I look at all things. How much I like what you write about St Francis! Yes, what we should seek for is indeed – is it not? – an exaltation and not an emancipation of the mind. The latter goes only with an abominable pride. Our ambition should lie not in revolt but in service.

'The news from Nîmes is so good, that it seems to me I have God's permission to give way to joy. The only shadow this summer is my poor father's condition. In spite of all my care he still keeps sad, or rather he relapses into sadness the moment I leave him to himself, and it becomes less and less easy to get him out of it. All the joys of nature that are about us speak a language which has become foreign to him; he no longer even makes any effort to understand it. Miss Ashburton is well. I read your letters aloud to them both; each one gives us enough to talk about for three days, and then comes a fresh one.

'Robert left us the day before yesterday. He is going to spend the rest of his holidays with his friend R—, whose father is at the head of a model farm. Certainly the life we lead here is not very amusing for him. I could only encourage him in his idea when he spoke of leaving.

'. . . I have so much to say to you. I thirst for a talk, such an endless talk! Sometimes I can find no words, no distinct ideas – this evening I am writing as in a dream – and all I realize is an almost oppressive sense of infinite riches to bestow and to receive.

'How did we manage to be silent during so many long months? No doubt we were hibernating. Oh! may that frightful winter of our silence be for ever past! Now that I have found you again, life, thought, our souls – everything seems beautiful, adorable, inexhaustibly fertile.

'12th September.

'I have got your letter from Pisa. The weather is splendid here, too. Never before have I thought Normandy so beautiful. The day before yesterday I took an enormously long walk, going across country at random. When I came in I was not so much tired as excited, almost intoxicated with sun and joy. How beautiful the haystacks were in the burning sun! There was no need to imagine myself in Italy for me to think everything I saw wonderful.

'Yes, dear friend, it is as you say, an exhortation to joy which I hear and understand in Nature's "mingled hymn". I hear it in every bird's song; I breathe it in the scent of every flower, and I have reached the point of conceiving adoration as the only form of prayer, repeating over and over again with St Francis: "My God! My God! *e non altro*" – and nothing else – my heart filled with *inexpressible* love.

'Don't be afraid, though, of my becoming an ignoramus. I have been reading a great deal lately; with the help of a few rainy days I have, as it were, folded my adoration up into my books. Finished Malebranche and began at once on Leibnitz' *Letters to Clarke*. Then, as a rest, read Shelley's *Cenci* – without pleasure; read *The Sensitive Plant* too. I shall make you very indignant, but I would give nearly all Shelley and all Byron for Keats' four odes, which we read together last summer; just as I would give all Hugo for a few of Baudelaire's sonnets. The words "great poet" have no meaning – what is important is to be a *pure* poet. Oh, my brother! thank you for having taught me to understand and love these things.

'No, don't cut short your journey for the sake of a few days' meeting. Seriously, it is better that we should not see each other again just yet. Believe me, if you were with me I could not think of you more. I should be sorry to give you pain, but I have come to the point of no longer wanting your presence – now. Shall I confess? If I knew you were coming this evening I should fly away.

'Oh! don't ask me to explain this feeling, please, I only know that I think of you unceasingly (which ought to be enough for *your* happiness) and that I am happy so.'

*

A short time after this last letter, and immediately after my return from Italy, I was called up for my military service and sent to Nancy. I did not know a living soul there, but I was glad to be alone, for it was thus more clearly apparent to my lover's pride and to Alissa herself, that her letters were my only refuge, and that the thought of her was, as Ronsard would have said, 'my only entelechy'.

To tell the truth I bore the pretty severe discipline to which we were subjected very cheerily. I stiffened myself to endurance, and in my letters to Alissa complained only of absence. We even found in this long separation a trial worthy of our valour. 'You who never complain,' wrote Alissa: 'you whom I cannot imagine faltering.' What would I not have endured to prove the truth of her words?

Almost a year had gone by since our last meeting. She seemed not to consider this, but to count her time of waiting only from now onwards. I reproached her with it.

'Was I not with you in Italy?' she replied. 'Ungrateful! I never left you for a single day. You must understand that now, for a time, I can't follow you any longer, and it is that, only that, which I call separation. I try hard, it is true, to imagine you as a soldier. I can't succeed. At best I see you in the evening in your little room in the Rue Gambetta, writing or reading – but no, not even that! In reality it is only at Fongueusemare or Le Havre that I can see you, in a year from now.

'A year! I don't count the days that have already gone by, my hope fastens its gaze on that point in the future, which is slowly, slowly, drawing nearer. Do you remember the low wall that shelters the chrysanthemums, at the end of the garden, and how sometimes we used to venture along the top of it? Juliette and you walked on it as boldly as though you were Mussulmans going straight to Paradise; as for me, I was seized with giddiness after the first step or two, and you used to call to me from below, "Don't look at your feet! Eyes front! Don't stop! Look at the goal!" And then, at last – and it was more of a help than your words – you would climb on to the wall at the other end and wait for me. Then I no longer trembled; I no longer felt giddy; I no longer saw anything but you; I ran until I reached your open arms.

'Without faith in you, Jerome, what would become of me? I have need to feel you strong; need to lean on you. Don't weaken.'

Out of a sort of spirit of defiance, which made us deliberately prolong our time of waiting – out of fear, too, of an unsatisfactory meeting – we agreed that I should spend my few days' leave at Christmas with Miss Ashburton, in Paris.

I have already told you that I do not give all her letters. Here is one I received about the middle of February:

'Great excitement the day before yesterday in passing along the Rue de Paris to see Abel's book, very ostentatiously displayed in M—'s shop window. You had indeed announced its appearance, but I could not believe in its *reality*. I wasn't able to resist going in; but the title seemed to me so ridiculous that I hesitated to name it to the shopman; I was, in fact, on the point of going out again with any other book, no matter what. Fortunately a little pile of *Wantonness* was set out for customers near the counter, and I took a copy and put down my money, without having had to speak.

'I am grateful to Abel for not having sent me his book! I have not been able to look through it without shame; shame, not so much because of the book itself – in which, after all, I see more folly than indecency – but shame to think that Abel, Abel Vautier, your friend, should have written it. I searched in vain, from page to page, for the "great talent" which the *Temps* reviewer has discovered in it. In our little society of Le Havre, where Abel is often mentioned, people say that the book is very successful. I hear his incurable futility of mind called "lightness" and "grace"; of course, I keep prudently silent, and have told no one but you that I have read it. Poor Pasteur Vautier, who at first looked deeply grieved – and very rightly – is now beginning to wonder whether, instead, he hasn't cause to feel proud; and all his acquaintance are doing their best to persuade him so. Yesterday, at Aunt Plantier's, when Mme V— said to him abruptly: "You must be very happy, Pasteur, over your son's wonderful success!" he answered rather abashed, "Oh! I haven't got as far as that yet!" "But you will! But you will!" said Aunt, innocently no doubt, but in such an encouraging voice that everyone began to laugh, even he.

'What will it be when *The New Abelard* is brought out? I hear it is going to be acted at some theatre or other on the Boulevards, and that the papers are beginning to talk of it already! Poor Abel! Is that really the success he wants? Will he be satisfied with that?

'Yesterday in the *Interior Consolation* I read these words: "All human glory, indeed all temporal honour, all wordly grandeur, compared with Thy eternal glory, is vanity and foolishness." And I thought, "Oh, God! I thank Thee that Thou hast chosen Jerome for Thy celestial glory, compared with which the other is vanity and foolishness."'

The weeks and months went by in monotonous occupations; but as there was nothing on which I could fasten my thoughts but memories or hopes, I hardly noticed how slow the time was, how long the hours.

My uncle and Alissa were to go in June to the neighbourhood of Nîmes on a visit to Juliette, who was expecting her baby about that time. Less favourable news of her health made them hasten their departure.

'Your last letter, addressed to Le Havre' [wrote Alissa], 'arrived after we had left. I cannot explain by what accident it reached me here only a week later. During all that week I went about with a soul that was only half a soul, a shivering, pitiful, beggarly soul. Oh, my brother! I am only truly myself – more than myself – when I am with you.

'Juliette is better again. We are daily expecting her confinement, without undue anxiety. She knows that I am writing to you this morning. The day after our arrival at Aigues-Vives, she said to me: "And Jerome? What has become of him? Does he write to you still?" And as I couldn't but tell her the truth: "When you write to him," she said, "tell him that . . ." she hesitated a moment, and then, smiling very sweetly, went on: "that I am cured." I was rather afraid that in her letters, which are always so gay, she might be acting a part and taking herself in by it. The things she makes her happiness out of nowadays are so different from the things she had dreamt of, the things on which it seemed her happiness ought to have depended!
. . . Ah! this, that we call *happiness*, how intimate a part of the soul it is, and of what little importance are the outside elements which seem to go to its making! I spare you all the reflections I make during my walks along the *garrigue*, when what astonishes me most is that I don't feel happier; Juliette's happiness ought to fill me with joy . . . why does my heart give way to an incomprehensible melancholy against which I am unable to fight? The very beauty of the country, which I feel, which at any rate I recognize, adds still further to this inexplicable sadness. When you wrote to me from Italy, I was able to see everything through you; now I feel as if I were depriving you of whatever I look at without you. And then at Fongueusemare or at Le Havre I had made myself a kind of rough-weather virtue, for use on rainy days; here, this virtue seems out of place; and I feel uneasily that there is no occasion for it. The laughter of the people and of the country jars upon me; perhaps what I call being sad is simply not being so noisy as they. No doubt there was some pride in my joy formerly, for at present, in the midst of this alien gaiety, what I feel is not unlike humiliation.

'I have scarcely been able to pray since I have been here: I have the childish feeling that God is no longer in the same place. Good-bye; I must stop now. I am ashamed of this blasphemy, and of my weakness,

74

and of my sadness, and of confessing them, and of writing you all this which I should tear up tomorrow if it were not posted tonight. . . .'

The next letter spoke only of the birth of her niece, whose godmother she was to be, of Juliette's joy and of my uncle's, but of her own feelings there was no further question.

Then there were letters dated from Fongueusemare again, where Juliette came to stay with her in July.

'Édouard and Juliette left us this morning. It is my little niece whom I regret most; when I see her again in six months' time I shall no longer recognize every one of her movements; she had scarcely one which I hadn't seen her invent. Growth is always so mysterious and surprising; it is through failure of attention that we are not oftener astonished at it. How many hours I have spent, bending over the little cradle, where so many hopes lie centred. By what selfishness, by what conceit, by what lack of desire for improvement is it that development ceases so soon, and that every creature becomes definitive, when still so far from God? Oh! if we could, if we would but approach nearer to Him . . . think, what emulation!

'Juliette seems very happy. I was grieved at first to find that she had given up her piano and her reading, but Édouard Teissières doesn't like music and hasn't much taste for books; no doubt Juliette is acting wisely in not seeking her pleasure where he cannot follow her. On the other hand, she takes an interest in her husband's occupations and he tells her all about his business. It has developed greatly this year; it pleases him to say that it is because of his marriage, which has brought him an important *clientèle* at Le Havre. Robert accompanied him the last time he went on a business journey. Édouard is very kind to him, declares he understands his character and doesn't despair of seeing him take seriously to this kind of work.

'Father is much better; the sight of his daughter's happiness has made him young again; he is interesting himself again in the farm and the garden, and has just asked me to go on with our reading aloud, which we had begun with Miss Ashburton and which was interrupted by the Teissières' visit. I am reading them Baron Hübner's travels, and enjoy them very much myself. I shall have more time for my own reading too; but I want some advice from you; this morning I took up several books, one after the other, without feeling a taste for any of them!'

Alissa's letters, henceforward, became more troubled, more pressing.

'The fear of troubling you prevents me from telling you how much I want you,' [she wrote towards the end of the summer]. 'Every day that has to be got through before I see you again weighs on me, oppresses me. Another two months. It seems longer than all the rest of the time which has already gone by without you! Everything I take up to while away the hours, seems nothing but an absurd stop-gap, and I cannot set myself to anything. My books are without virtue and without charm; my walks have no attraction; Nature has lost her glamour; the garden is emptied of colour, of scent.

'I envy you your fatigue-parties and your compulsory drills which are constantly dragging you out of yourself, tiring you, hurrying along your days, and, at night, flinging you, wearied out, to your sleep. The stirring description you gave me of the manoeuvres haunts me. For the last few nights I have been sleeping badly, and several times I have been awakened with a start by the bugles sounding reveille . . . I actually heard them. I can so well imagine the intoxication of which you speak, the morning rapture, the lightheadedness almost . . . How beautiful the plateau of Malzéville must have been in the icy radiance of dawn!

'This is my last letter, my friend. However uncertain the date of your return may be, it cannot be delayed much longer. I shall not be able to write to you any more. I should have preferred our meeting to have been at Fongueusemare, but the weather has broken; it is very cold, and father talks of nothing but going back to town. Now that Juliette and Robert are no longer with us we could easily take you in, but it is better that you should go to Aunt Félicie, who will be glad, too, to have you.

'As the day of our meeting comes near, I look forward to it with growing anxiety, almost with apprehension. I seem now to dread your coming that I so longed for; I try not to think of it; I imagine your ring at the bell, your step on the stairs, and my heart stops beating or hurts me. . . . And whatever you do, don't expect me to be able to speak to you. I feel my past comes to an end here; I see nothing beyond; my life stops. . . .'

Four days later, however – a week, that is, before I was liberated from my military service – I received one more letter, a very short one:

'My friend, I entirely approve of your not wanting to prolong beyond measure your stay at Le Havre and the time of our first meeting. What should we have to say to each other that we have not already written? So if the business connected with your examination calls you to Paris as early as the 28th, don't hesitate, don't even regret that you are not able to give us more than two days. Shall we not have all our lives?'

6

IT was at Aunt Plantier's that our first meeting took place. I suddenly felt that my military service had made me heavy and clumsy. ... Later on I thought she must have found me altered. But why should this first deceptive impression have had any importance for us two? As for me, I was so much afraid of not recognizing the Alissa I knew, that at first I hardly dared look at her. No! what was really embarrassing was the absurd position of being engaged which they all forced upon us, and everybody's anxiety to leave us alone and hurry away when we were there!

'Oh, Aunt! you are not the least in the way; we have nothing private to say to each other,' cried Alissa at last, impatient at the tactless manner in which the excellent women tried to efface herself.

'Yes, yes! my dears. I quite understand. When young people haven't seen each other for a long time, they always have lots of little things to tell each other.'

'Please, Aunt! You really will annoy us if you go away!' and this was said in a tone which was almost angry, and in which I hardly recognized Alissa's voice.

'Aunt! I assure you that if you go away, we shan't utter a single other word!' added I, laughing, but myself filled with a certain apprehension at the idea of our being left alone. And then, with sham cheerfulness, we all three set to work to make conversation, trying to hide our embarrassment beneath the forced liveliness of our commonplace talk. We were to meet again the next day, as my uncle had invited me to lunch, so that we parted that evening without regret, glad to put an end to this absurd scene.

I arrived long before luncheon-time, but I found Alissa talking to a girl friend, whom she had not the strength of mind to send away, and who was not discreet enough to go. When at last she left us, I pretended to be surprised that Alissa had not kept her to lunch. We were both of us in a state of nervous tension and tired by a sleepless night. My uncle appeared. Alissa felt that I thought him aged. He had grown rather deaf, and heard my voice with difficulty; the necessity I was under of shouting so as to make myself understood made my talk dull and stupid.

After lunch Aunt Plantier, as had been arranged, came to take us out in her carriage; she drove us to Orcher, with the idea of letting Alissa and me do the pleasantest part of the journey on foot.

The weather was hot for the time of the year. The part of the hill up which we had to walk was exposed to the sun and unattractive; the leafless trees gave us no shelter. In our anxiety to rejoin the carriage in which our aunt was to wait for us, we hastened our pace uncomfortably. My head was aching so badly that I could not extract a single idea from it; to keep myself in countenance, or because I thought that the gesture might serve instead of words, I had taken Alissa's hand, which she let me keep. Our emotion, the rapidity of our walk, and the awkwardness of our silence, sent the blood to our faces; I felt my temples throbbing; Alissa's colour was unpleasantly heightened; and soon the discomfort of feeling the contact of our damp hands made us unclasp them and let them drop sadly to our sides.

We had made too much haste, and arrived at the cross-roads long before the carriage, which had taken another road and driven very slowly, because of my aunt's desire to leave us plenty of time for talking. We sat down on the bank at the side of the road; a cold wind, which suddenly got up, chilled us to the bone, for we were bathed in perspiration; then we walked on to meet the carriage. But the worst was again the pressing solicitude of our poor aunt, who was convinced that we had had a long and satisfactory talk and was longing to question us about our engagement. Alissa, unable to bear it, and with her eyes full of tears, alleged a violent headache, and we drove home in silence.

The next day I woke up with aching limbs and a bad chill, so unwell that I put off going to the Bucolins' till the afternoon. By ill luck, Alissa was not alone. Madeleine Plantier, one of Aunt Félicie's granddaughters, was there. I knew Alissa liked talking to her. She was staying with her grandmother for a few days, and when I came in, she exclaimed:

'If you are going back to the Côte when you leave here, we might as well go together.'

I agreed mechanically; so that I was unable to see Alissa alone. But the presence of this charming girl was, no doubt, a help to us; I no longer felt the intolerable embarrassment of the day before; the conversation between the three of us was soon going smoothly, and was less futile than I had at first feared. Alissa smiled strangely when I said good-bye to her; I had the impression that she had not understood till that moment that I was going away the next morning. But the prospect of my speedy return took away any touch of tragedy from my good-bye.

After dinner, however, prompted by a vague uneasiness, I went down to the town, where I wandered about for nearly an hour before I made up my mind to ring at the Bucolins' door. It was my uncle who received me. Alissa, who was not feeling very well, had already gone to her room and, no doubt, straight to bed. I talked to my uncle for a few moments, and then left.

It would be vain for me to blame the perverseness of these incidents, unfortunate though they were. For even if everything had favoured us, we should still have invented our embarrassment ourselves. But nothing could have made me more wretched than that Alissa, too, should feel this. This is the letter I received as soon as I got to Paris:

'My friend, what a melancholy meeting! You seemed to lay the blame on other people, but without being able to convince yourself. And now I think – I know – it will be so always. Oh! I beg of you, don't let us see each other again!

'Why this awkwardness, this feeling of being in a false position, this paralysis, this dumbness, when we have everything in the world to say to each other? The first day of your return this very silence made me happy, because I believed it would vanish, and that you would tell me the most wonderful things; it was impossible that you should leave me without.

'But when our lugubrious expedition to Orcher came to an end without a word, when, above all, our hands unclasped and fell apart so hopelessly, I thought my heart would have fainted within me for grief and pain. And what distressed me most was not so much that your hand let go mine, but my feeling that if yours had not, mine would have done so, for my hand too no longer felt happy in yours.

'The next day – yesterday – I expected you, madly, all the morning. I was too restless to stop indoors, and I left a line for you to tell you where to find me on the jetty. I stayed a long time looking at the stormy sea, but I was too miserable looking at it without you; I imagined suddenly that you were waiting for me in my room, and went in. I knew I shouldn't be free in the afternoon; Madeleine had told me the day before that she meant to come, and as I expected to see you in the morning I did not put her off. But, perhaps, it was to her presence we owed the only pleasant moments of our meeting. For a few minutes I had the strange illusion that this comfortable conversation was going to last a long, long time. And when you came up to the sofa where I was sitting beside her, and bent down and said "good-bye", I could not answer; it seemed as though it were the end of everything; it suddenly dawned upon me that you were going.

'You had no sooner left with Madeleine, than it struck me as impossible, unbearable. Will you believe it? I went out! I wanted to speak to you again, to tell you all the things I had not told you; I was already hurrying to the Plantiers' . . . It was late; I didn't have time, didn't dare . . . I came in again, desperate, to write to you – that I didn't want to write to you any more – a good-bye letter because I felt too much that our correspondence was nothing but a vast mirage, that we were each writing, alas! only to ourselves and that – Jerome! Jerome! Ah! how far apart we were all the time!

'I tore that letter up, it is true; but now I am writing it over again, almost the same. Oh! I do not love you less, my dear! On the contrary,

I never before felt so clearly, by my very disturbance, by my embarrassment as soon as you came near me, how deeply I loved you; but hopelessly too, for I must perforce confess it to myself – when you were away, I loved you more. I had already begun to suspect so, alas! This longed-for meeting has finally shown me the truth, and you, too, my friend, must needs be convinced of it. Good-bye, my much-loved brother; may God keep and guide you! To Him alone can we draw near with impunity.'

And as if this letter were not sufficiently painful, the next day she had added the following postscript:

'I do not wish to let this letter go without asking you to show a little more discretion in regard to what concerns us both. Many a time you have wounded me by talking to Juliette or Abel about things which should have remained private between you and me, and this is, indeed, what made me think – long before you suspected it – that your love was above all intellectual, the beautiful tenacity of a tender faithful mind.'

The fear lest I should show this letter to Abel had doubtless inspired the last lines. What suspicious instinct had put her on her guard? Had she formerly detected in my words some reflection of my friend's advice?

In truth, I felt myself far enough away from him! The paths we followed were henceforth divergent; and there was little need of these recommendations to teach me to bear the anxious burden of my grief alone.

The next three days were wholly occupied by my pleading; I wished to reply to Alissa; I was afraid of incurably inflaming the wound by too deliberate a discussion, by too vehement protestations, by the slightest clumsy word; twenty times over I began the letter in which my love struggled for its life. I cannot to this day re-read, without weeping, the tear-stained paper, which is the copy of the one I at last decided to send:

'Alissa! Have pity on me, on us both! Your letter hurts me. How much I wish I could smile at your fears! Yes, I felt everything you write; but I was afraid to own it to myself. What frightful reality you give to what is merely imaginary, and how you thicken it between us!

'If you feel that you love me less ... Ah! let me dismiss this cruel supposition, which your whole letter contradicts! But then, of what importance are your fleeting apprehensions? Alissa! As soon as I begin to argue, my words freeze; I can only hear the weeping of my heart. I love you too much to be skilful, and the more I love you the less I know what to say to you. "Intellectual love " ... what am I to answer to that? When it is with my whole soul that I love you, how can I distinguish between my intellect and my heart? But since our correspondence is the cause of your unkind imputation, since we have been so grievously hurt by our fall into reality from the heights to which that correspondence had raised us, since, if you were to write to me now you would think that you were writing only to yourself, since, too, I have not strength to bear another letter like your last – please, for a time, let us stop all communication.'

In the rest of my letter I protested and appealed against her judgement, imploring her to grant us the opportunity of another interview. The last had had everything against it; the scene, the personages, the time of year – and even our correspondence, whose impassioned tone had prepared us for it with so little prudence. This time it should be preceded only by silence. I wished it to take place in the spring, at Fongueusemare, where my uncle would let me stay during the Easter holidays, for as long or as short a time as she herself should think fit.

My determination was firmly taken, and as soon as my letter had gone I was able to bury myself in my work.

*

I was to see Alissa once more before the end of the year. Miss Ashburton, whose health had been declining for some months past, died four days before Christmas. On my return from my military service I had gone back to stay with her. I left her very little and was present at her last moments. A card from Alissa showed me that our vow of silence lay nearer her heart than my

83

bereavement; she would come up, she said, for the day, just to go to the funeral, which my uncle would not be able to attend.

She and I were almost the only mourners to be present at the burial service and afterwards to follow the coffin. We walked side by side and exchanged barely a few sentences; but in church where she took her seat beside me, I several times felt her eyes resting tenderly upon me.

'It is agreed,' said she, as she left me, 'nothing before Easter.'

'No, but at Easter . . .'

'I will expect you.'

We were at the gate of the cemetery. I suggested taking her to the station; but she called a cab and without a word of farewell, left me.

7

'ALISSA is waiting for you in the garden,' said my uncle, after having embraced me paternally, when one day at the end of April I arrived at Fongueusemare. If at first I was disappointed at not finding her ready to welcome me, the next moment I was grateful that she had spared us both the first commonplace greetings.

She was at the bottom of the garden. I made my way to the place at the head of the steps, where, at this time of year, the shrubs that set it closely round were all in flower – lilacs, rowan trees, laburnums, and weigelias: in order not to catch sight of her from too far, or so that she should not see me coming, I took the other side of the garden, along the shady path, where the air was cool beneath the branches.

I advanced slowly; the sky was like my joy – warm, bright, delicately pure. No doubt she was expecting me by the other path. I was close to her, behind her, before she heard me; I stopped . . . and as if time could have stopped with me, 'This is the moment,' thought I, 'the most delicious moment, perhaps, of all, even though it should precede happiness itself – which happiness itself will not equal.'

I meant to fall on my knees before her; I took a step which she heard. She got up suddenly, letting the embroidery at which she was working roll to the ground; she stretched out her arms towards me, put her hands on my shoulders. For a few moments we stayed so, with her arms outstretched, her face smiling and bent towards me, looking at me tenderly without speaking. She was dressed all in white. On her grave face – almost too grave – I recognized her childhood's smile.

'Listen, Alissa,' I cried suddenly. 'I have twelve days before me. I will not stay one more than you please. Let us settle on a sign, which shall mean: "Tomorrow you must leave

Fongueusemare." The next day I will go, without recrimination, without complaint. Do you agree?'

As I had not prepared what I was going to say, I spoke more easily. She reflected a moment; then:

'The evening that I come down to dinner without wearing the amethyst cross you like ... will you understand?'

'That is to be my last evening.'

'But will you be able to go without a tear or a sigh?'

'Without a good-bye. I will leave you on that last evening exactly as I shall have done the evening before, so simply that you will wonder whether I have understood. But when you look for me the next morning, I shall just not be there.'

'I shall not look for you the next morning.'

She held out her hand; as I raised it to my lips, I added:

'But from now till the fatal evening, not an allusion to make me feel that it is coming.'

'And you, not an allusion to the parting that will follow.'

The embarrassment, which the solemnity of this meeting was in danger of creating between us, had now to be dispelled.

'I should so much like,' I went on, 'that these few days with you should seem like other days ... I mean that we should not feel, either of us, that they are exceptional. And then ... if we were not to try too hard to talk just at first ...'

She began to laugh. I added:

'Isn't there anything we could do together?'

Ever since we could remember we had taken great pleasure in gardening. An inexperienced gardener had lately replaced the old one, and there was a great deal to be done in the garden, which had been neglected for the last two months. Some of the rose trees had been badly pruned; some, luxuriant growers, were encumbered with dead wood; some of the ramblers had come down for want of the necessary props; others were being exhausted by suckers. Most of them had been grafted by us; we recognized our nurslings; the attention of which they were in need took up a large part of our time, and allowed us during the first three days to talk a great deal without saying anything of weight, and, when we said nothing, it enabled us not to feel our silence burdensome.

In this way we once more grew accustomed to one another. It was on this familiarity that I counted, rather than on any actual explanation. The very recollection of our separation was already beginning to disappear from between us, and the fearfulness which I used to feel in her, the tension of spirit which she used to fear in me, were already beginning to grow less. Alissa seemed younger than during my melancholy visit of the autumn, and I had never thought her prettier. I had not yet kissed her. Every evening I saw sparkling on her bodice the little amethyst cross, which she wore hanging from a gold chain round her neck. Hope sprang up again, confidently, in my breast. Hope, do I say? No! it was already certainty, and I thought I felt it too in Alissa; for I was so little doubtful of myself that I could no longer have any doubts of her. Little by little our talk grew bolder.

'Alissa,' I said to her one morning, when all the air breathed laughter and delight and our hearts were opening like the flowers, 'now that Juliette is happy, won't you let us too ...'

I spoke slowly, with my eyes fixed upon her; on a sudden she turned pale, so extraordinarily, that I could not finish my sentence.

'Dear!' she began, without turning her eyes towards me, 'I feel happier with you than I thought it was possible to feel ... but, believe me, we were not born for happiness.'

'What can the soul prefer to happiness?' I cried, impetuously. She whispered:

'Holiness ...' so low that I divined rather than heard the word.

My whole happiness spread its wings and flew away out of my heart and up to Heaven.

'I cannot reach it without you,' I said, and with my head

on her knees, weeping like a child – but for love, not for grief –
I repeated again and again: 'Not without you; not without
you!'

Then that day, too, passed by like the others. But in the
evening Alissa came down without the little amethyst ornament. Faithful to my promise, the next morning at daybreak
I left.

On the following day I received the strange letter which I
give below, with these lines of Shakespeare's as motto:

> 'That strain again, – it had a dying fall;
> Oh, it came o'er my ear like the sweet sound,
> That breathes upon a bank of violets,
> Stealing and giving odour. – Enough; no more,
> 'Tis not so sweet now as it was before.

'Yes! In spite of myself, I looked for you the whole morning, my
brother. I could not believe that you had gone. I felt resentful against
you for having kept to our engagement. I thought it must be a jest.
I expected you to step out from behind every bush. But no! you have
really gone. Thank you.

'I spent the rest of the day haunted by the constant presence of
thoughts, which I should like to communicate to you, and by the
peculiar and very definite fear that if I did not, I should have the
feeling later on of having failed in my duty towards you, of having
deserved your reproaches . . .

'In the first moments of your stay at Fongueusemare it was astonishment that I felt – soon after it was uneasiness – at the strange contentment that filled my whole being in your presence; "a contentment so
great," you said, "that I desire nothing beyond!" Alas! that is just
what makes me uneasy. . . .

'I am afraid, my friend, lest you should misunderstand me. Above
all, I am afraid lest you should take for subtlety (Oh, how mistaken a
subtlety!) what is merely the expression of the most violent feeling
of my soul.

'"If it did not suffice, it would not be happiness," you said, do you
remember? And I did not know what to answer. No, Jerome, it does
not suffice us. Jerome, it must not suffice us. I cannot take this delicious

contentment for the true one. Did we not realize last autumn what misery it covered over! . . .

'The true one! Ah! God forbid! We were born for a happiness other than that. . . .

'Just as it was our correspondence which spoilt our meeting last autumn, so now the memory of your presence yesterday disenchants my letter of today. What has happened to the delight I used to take in writing to you? By writing to each other, by being with each other, we have exhausted all that is pure in the joy to which our love dares aspire. And now, in spite of myself, I exclaim, like Orsino in *Twelfth Night*: "Enough, no more; 'tis not so sweet now as it was before."

'Good-bye, my friend. *Hic incipit amor Dei*. Ah! will you ever know how much I love you? . . . Until the end I will be your

'ALISSA.'

Against the snare of virtue I was defenceless. All heroism attracted and dazzled me, for I could not separate it from love. Alissa's letter inspired me with a rash and intoxicating enthusiasm. God knows that I strove after more virtue only for her sake. Any path, provided it climbed upwards, would lead me to her. Ah! The ground could not too soon narrow enough to hold only her and me! Alas! I did not suspect the subtlety of her feint, and little imagined that it would be by a height where there was room for only one, that she might escape me once more.

I replied lengthily. I remember the only passage of my letter that was at all clear-sighted.

'I often think,' I said, 'that my love is the best part of me: that all my virtues are suspended to it; that it raises me above myself, and that without it I should fall back to the mediocre level of a very ordinary disposition. It is the hope of reaching you that will always make me think the steepest path the best.'

What did I add which could have induced her to answer as follows:

'But, my friend, holiness is not a choice; it is an obligation' [the word was underlined three times in her letter]. 'If you are what I take you to be, *you* will not be able to evade it either.'

That was all. I understood, or rather I had a foreboding, that our correspondence would stop there, and that neither the most cunning counsels nor the most steadfast determination would be of any avail.

I wrote again, however, lengthily, tenderly. After my third letter I received this note:

'My friend,
'Do not imagine that I have made any resolution not to write to you; I merely no longer take any pleasure in writing. And yet your letters still interest me, but I reproach myself more and more for engrossing so much of your thoughts.

'The summer is not far off. I propose that we give up our correspondence for a time, and that you come and spend the last fortnight of September with me at Fongueusemare. Do you accept? If you do, I have no need of a reply. I shall take your silence for consent, and hope, therefore, that you will not answer.'

I did not answer. No doubt this silence was only the last trial to which she was subjecting me. When, after a few months' work and a few weeks' travel, I returned to Fongueusemare, it was with the most tranquil assurance.

How should I, by a simple recital, make clear at once what I myself understood at first so ill? What can I paint here save the occasion of the wretchedness which from that moment overwhelmed me wholly? For if I have no forgiveness in my heart today for my failure to recognize that love that was still throbbing, hidden under a semblance so artificial, it was at first only this semblance that I was able to see; and so, no longer finding my friend, I accused her . . . No! Even then, Alissa, I did not accuse you, but wept despairingly that I could recognize you no longer. Now that I can gauge the strength of your love by the cunning of its silence and by its cruel workings, must I love you all the more, the more agonizingly you bereft me?

Disdain? Coldness? No; nothing that could be overcome;

nothing against which I could even struggle: and sometimes I hesitated, doubting whether I had not invented my misery, so subtle seemed its cause, and so skilful was Alissa's pretence of not understanding it. What should I have complained of? Her welcome was more smiling than ever; never had she shown herself more cordial, more attentive; the first day I was almost taken in by it. What did it matter, after all, that she did her hair in a new way, which flattened it and dragged it back from her face, so that her features were harshened and their true expression altered – that an unbecoming dress, dull in colour and ugly in texture, turned the delicate rhythm of her body to clumsiness? . . . There was nothing here, I thought blindly, that might not be remedied the very next day, either of her own accord or at my request. I was more unpleasantly affected by the cordiality, by the attentions, which were so foreign to our habits, and in which I was afraid I saw more deliberation than spontaneity, and, though I scarcely dare say so, more politeness than love.

That evening, when I went into the drawing-room, I was astonished not to find the piano in its usual place; Alissa answered my exclamation of disappointment in her most tranquil voice:

'It has gone to be done up, dear.'

'But I repeatedly told you, my child,' said my uncle, in a tone of reproach that was almost severe, 'that as it had done well enough up till now, you might have waited until Jerome had gone before sending it away; your haste has deprived us of a great pleasure.'

'But, father,' said she, turning aside to blush, 'I assure you it had got so jingly latterly that Jerome himself wouldn't have been able to get anything out of it.'

'When you played it, it didn't seem so bad,' said my uncle.

She stayed a few moments in the shadow, stooping down, as if she were engaged in taking the measurements of a chair cover, then she left the room abruptly, and did not return till later, when she brought in the tray with the cup of *tisane* which my uncle was in the habit of taking every evening.

The next day she changed neither the way of doing her hair nor her dress; seated beside her father on a bench in front of the house, she went on with the mending on which she had already been engaged the evening before. On the bench or the table beside her was a great basket full of stockings and socks into which she dipped. A few days later it was towels and sheets. This work absorbed her, it seemed, to such a pitch that every gleam of expression vanished from her lips and her eyes.

'Alissa!' I exclaimed the first evening, almost terrified by this obliteration of all poetry from her face, which I could hardly recognize, and at which I had been gazing for some moments without her seeming to feel my look.

'What is it?' said she, raising her head.

'I wanted to see if you would hear me. Your thoughts seemed so far away from me.'

'No; they are here; but this darning requires a great deal of attention.'

'Would you like me to read to you while you are sewing?'

'I am afraid I shouldn't be able to listen very well.'

'Why do you choose such absorbing work to do?'

'Someone must do it.'

'There are so many poor women who would be glad to do it for the sake of earning a trifle. It can't be from economy that you undertake such a tedious task?'

She at once assured me that she liked no other kind of sewing so much, that it was the only kind she had done for a long time past, and that she was doubtless out of practice for doing anything else. She smiled as she spoke. Never had her voice been sweeter than now, when she was so grieving me. 'I am saying nothing but what is natural,' her face seemed to declare, 'why should it make you sad?'

And my whole heart's protest no longer even rose to my lips – it choked me.

A day or two later, as we had been picking roses, she invited me to carry them for her to her room, into which I had not as yet been this year. What flattering hopes arose in me at once! For I had not got beyond blaming myself for my sadness; one word from her would have healed my heart.

I never went into this room without emotion; I cannot tell what it was that made up the kind of melodious peace which breathed in it, and in which I recognized Alissa. The blue shadow of the curtains at the windows and round the bed, the furniture of shining mahogany, the order, the spotlessness, the silence, all spoke to my heart of her purity and pensive grace.

I was astonished that morning to see that two large photographs of some Masaccios, which I had brought back from Italy, were no longer on the wall beside her bed; I was on the point of asking her what had become of them when my glance fell on the bookshelf close by, where she used to keep her bedside books. This little collection had been gradually formed, partly by the books I had given her, partly by others which we had read together. I had just noticed that all these books had been removed, and that they had been replaced exclusively by a number of insignificant little works of vulgar piety, for which I hoped she had nothing but contempt. Raising my eyes suddenly, I saw that Alissa was laughing – yes, laughing – as she watched me.

'I beg your pardon,' said she at once: 'your face made me laugh; it fell so abruptly when you saw my bookcase.'

I felt very little inclined for pleasantry.

'No, really, Alissa, is that what you read now?'

'Yes, certainly. What is it surprises you?'

'I should have thought that a mind accustomed to substantial food would have been disgusted by such sickly stuff.'

'I don't understand you,' said she. 'These are humble souls who talk to me simply, and express themselves as best they can. I take pleasure in their society. I know beforehand that they will not fall into any snare of fine language, and that I, as I read, shall not be tempted by any profane admiration.'

'Do you read nothing but that, then, now?'

'Almost. Yes, for the last few months. But I haven't much time for reading now. And I confess that quite lately, when I tried to re-read one of the great authors whom you taught me to admire, I felt like the man in the Scriptures, who strives to add a cubit to his height.'

'Who is this "great author" who has given you such an odd opinion of yourself?'

'He didn't give it me, but it was while reading him that I got it. . . . It was Pascal. Perhaps I lighted on some passage that was not so good. . . .'

I made an impatient movement. She spoke in a clear monotonous voice, as if she were reciting a lesson, not lifting her eyes from her flowers, which she went on arranging and rearranging interminably. She stopped for an instant at my movement and then continued in the same tone:

'Such surprising grandiloquence and such effort! – and to prove so little! I wonder sometimes whether his pathetic intonation is not the result of doubt rather than of faith. The voice of perfect faith speaks with fewer tears, with fewer tremors.'

'It is just those very tremors, those very tears which make the beauty of his voice,' I endeavoured to retort, although dispiritedly; for in her words I could recognize nothing of what I loved in Alissa. I write them down as I remember them, and without any after addition of either art or logic.

'If he had not first emptied this life of its joy,' she went on, 'it would weigh heavier in the balance than . . .'

'Than what?' I asked, for I was amazed at her strange sayings.

'Than the uncertain felicity he holds out.'

'Don't you believe in it, then?' I exclaimed.

'No matter!' she answered: 'I wish it to remain uncertain, so that every suspicion of a bargain may be removed. The soul that loves God steeps itself in virtue out of natural nobility, and not for the hope of reward.'

'And that is the reason of the secret scepticism in which nobility such as Pascal's finds a refuge?'

'Not scepticism – Jansenism,' said she smiling. 'What have I to do with such things? These poor souls, here,' she added, turning towards her books, 'would be at a loss to say whether they are Jansenist or quietist or what not. They bow down before God like the grass which is bent by the wind, without guile or anxiety or beauty. They consider themselves of little account, and know that their only value lies in their effacement before God.'

'Alissa!' I cried, 'why do you tear off your wings?' Her voice remained so calm and natural that my exclamation seemed to me all the more absurdly emphatic.

She smiled again, and shook her head. 'All that I brought away from my last visit to Pascal . . .'

'Was what?' I asked, for she stopped.

'This saying of Christ's: "Whosoever shall seek to save his life shall lose it." And as for that,' she went on, smiling still more and looking me steadily in the face, 'I really hardly understood him any longer. When one has lived any time in the society of such lowly ones as these, it is extraordinary how quickly the sublimity of the great leaves one breathless and exhausted.'

Would my discomposure allow me no answer?

'If I were obliged to read all these sermons and tracts with you now . . .'

'But,' she interrupted, 'I should be very sorry to see you read them! I agree with you; I think you were meant for much better things than that.'

She spoke quite simply and without seeming to suspect that my heart might be rent by these words which implied the separation of our lives. My head was burning; I should have liked to go on speaking; I should have liked to cry; perhaps my tears would have vanquished her; but I remained without saying a word, my elbows on the mantelpiece, my head buried in my hands. She went on calmly arranging her flowers, seeing nothing – or pretending to see nothing of my suffering. . . .

At this moment the first bell rang.

'I shall never be ready for lunch,' said she. 'You must go away now.' And as if it had been nothing but play: 'We will go on with this conversation another time.'

We never went on with the conversation. Alissa continually eluded me; not that she ever appeared to be avoiding me; but every casual occupation became a duty of far more urgent importance. I had to wait my turn; I only came after the constantly recurring cares of the household, after she had attended to the alterations that were being carried out in the barn, after her visits to the farmers, and after her visits to the poor, with whom she busied herself more and more. I had the time that was left over, and very little it was; I never saw her but she was in a hurry – though it was still, perhaps, in the midst of these trivial occupations, and when I gave up pursuing her, that I least felt how much I had been dispossessed. The slightest talk showed it me more clearly. When Alissa granted me a few minutes, it was, indeed, for the most laborious conversation to which she lent herself as one does to playing with a child. She passed beside me swiftly, absent-minded and smiling; and I felt she had become more distant than if I had never known her. It even seemed to me sometimes that there was a kind of challenge in her smile, or at any rate a kind of irony, and that she took amusement in thus eluding my wishes. . . . And at that it was myself that I turned to upbraid, not wishing to give way to reproaches, and, indeed, hardly knowing what might be expected from her, nor with what I could reproach her.

Thus the days from which I had promised myself so much

felicity passed by. I contemplated their flight with stupor, but without desiring to increase their number or delay their passage, so greatly each one aggravated my grief. Two days before my departure, however, Alissa came with me to the bench beside the deserted marl-pit; it was a bright autumn evening: as far as the cloudless horizon, every blue-tinted detail of the landscape stood out distinct and clear, and in the past the dimmest of its memories. I could not withhold my lamentations as I showed her my present unhappiness – as I showed her the happiness I had lost.

'But what is it I can do, my friend?' she said at once. 'You are in love with a phantom.'

'No, not with a phantom, Alissa.'

'With a creature of your imagination.'

'Alas! I am not inventing. She was once my friend. I call upon her. Alissa! Alissa! it was you I loved. What have you done with yourself? What have you made yourself become?'

She remained a few moments without answering, slowly pulling a flower to pieces and keeping her head down. Then, at last:

'Jerome, why don't you simply admit that you love me less?'

'Because it's not true! Because it's not true!' I exclaimed indignantly: 'because I never loved you more.'

'You love me – and yet you regret me!' she said, trying to smile, and slightly shrugging her shoulders.

'I cannot put my love into the past.'

The ground was giving way beneath me; and I caught at anything.

'It must pass with the rest.'

'A love like mine will pass only with me.'

'It will gradually grow less. The Alissa whom you think you still love, already exists only in your memory; a day will come when you will only remember that you loved her.'

'You speak as if her place might be taken in my heart, or as

if my heart were going to stop loving. Do you no longer remember that you once loved me yourself that you take such
pleasure in torturing me?'

I saw her pale lips tremble; in an almost inaudible voice she
whispered:

'No, no; Alissa has not changed in that.'

'Why, then nothing has changed,' I said, seizing her arm. . . .
She went on firmly:

'One word would explain everything; why don't you dare
say it?'

'What word?'

'I have grown older.'

'Hush!'

I protested immediately that I myself had grown as much
older as she, that the difference of age between us remained
the same . . . but she had regained control of herself; the one
and only moment had gone by, and by beginning to argue I
let slip my advantage; the ground gave way beneath me.

Two days later I left Fongueusemare, discontented with her
and with myself, full of a vague hatred against what I still called
'virtue', and of resentment against the habitual occupation
of my heart. It seemed as though during this last meeting, and
through the very exaggeration of my love, I had come to the
end of all my fervour; each one of Alissa's phrases, against
which I had at first rebelled, remained alive and triumphant
within me, after my protestations had died away. Yes, no
doubt, she was right! It was nothing but a phantom that I
cared for; the Alissa that I had loved, that I still loved, was no
more. . . . Yes, no doubt we had grown old! This frightful
obliteration of all poetry which had chilled my very heart,
was nothing, after all, but a return to the natural course of
things; if by slow degrees I had exalted her, if out of her I
had made myself an idol, and adorned it with all that I was
enamoured of, what now remained to me as the result of my

labours but my fatigue? As soon as she was left to herself, Alissa had relapsed to her own level – a mediocre level, on which I found myself too, but on which I no longer desired her. Ah! how absurd and fantastic seemed this exhausting effort of virtue in order to reach her there, on the heights where she had been placed by my own sole endeavour. A little less pride and our love would have been easy . . . but what sense was there in persisting in a love without object? This was to be obstinate, not to be faithful. Faithful to what? To a delusion. Was it not wiser to admit to myself that I had been mistaken?

In the meantime I had been offered a place in the School of Athens; I agreed to take it up at once, with no feeling of either ambition or pleasure, but welcoming the idea of departure as though it had been an escape.

8

AND yet I saw Alissa once more. It was three years later, towards the end of summer. Ten months before, I had heard from her the news of my uncle's death. A fairly long letter, which I had at once written her from Palestine, where I was travelling at the time, had remained unanswered.

Happening to be at Le Havre, on I forget what errand, a natural instinct set me on the road to Fongueusemare. I knew Alissa was there, but I was afraid she might not be alone. I had not announced my arrival; shrinking from the idea of presenting myself like an ordinary visitor, I went on my way undecided; should I go in? or should I go away without having seen her, without having tried to see her? Yes, without doubt, I would just walk up the avenue, sit on the bench where sometimes, perhaps, she still went to sit . . . and I was already beginning to wonder what token I could leave behind me, which after I had gone, would tell of my coming. . . . Thus reflecting, I walked slowly on; and now that I had resolved not to see her, the sharpness of the sorrow which wrung my heart began to give way to a melancholy that was almost sweet. I had already reached the avenue, and, for fear of being taken unawares, I was walking on the footpath which ran along the bottom of the bank skirting the farmyard. I knew a place on the bank from which one could look over into the garden; I climbed up; a gardener whom I did not recognize was raking one of the paths and soon disappeared from sight. There was a new gate to the courtyard. A dog barked as I went by. Further on, where the avenue came to an end, I turned to the right, came again upon the garden wall, and was making my way to the portion of the beech wood, parallel to the avenue I had left, when, as I was passing by the little door that led into the kitchen garden, the idea of going in suddenly seized me.

The door was shut. The inside bolt, however, offered only

a slight resistance and I was on the point of forcing it open with my shoulder. . . . At that moment I heard the sound of steps; I drew back round the corner of the wall.

I could not see who it was that came out of the garden; but I heard, I felt it was Alissa. She took three steps forward and called in a weak voice:

'Is that you, Jerome?'

My heart, which was beating violently, stopped, and as no word would come from my choking throat, she repeated louder:

'Jerome! Is that you?'

At hearing her call me in this way, the emotion which seized on me was so great that it forced me to my knees. As I still did not answer, Alissa took a few steps forward, turned the corner of the wall, and I suddenly felt her against me – against me, who was kneeling there hiding my face with my arm, as if in dread of seeing her too soon. She remained a few moments stooping over me, while I covered her frail hands with kisses.

'Why were you hiding?' she said, as simply as if those three years of absence had lasted only a few days.

'How did you guess it was I?'

'I was expecting you.'

'Expecting me?' said I, so astonished that I could only repeat her words, wondering . . . And as I was still on my knees:

'Let us go to the bench,' she went on. 'Yes, I knew I was to see you again once more. For the last three days I have come here every evening and called you, as I did tonight. . . . Why didn't you answer?'

'If you had not come upon me by surprise, I should have gone away without seeing you,' I said, steeling myself against the emotion which had at first overmastered me. 'I happened to be at Le Havre, and merely meant to walk along the avenue and round the outside of the garden and to rest a few moments on this bench, where I thought you might still come to sit sometimes, and then . . .'

'Look what I have brought here to read for the last three evenings,' she interrupted, and held out to me a packet of letters; I recognized those I had written her from Italy. At that moment I raised my eyes to look at her. She was extraordinarily changed; her thinness, her paleness smote my heart horribly. Leaning heavily upon my arm, she clung to me as though she were frightened or cold. She was still in deep mourning, and no doubt the black lace which she had put round her head, and which framed her face, added to her paleness. She was smiling, but her failing limbs seemed hardly to bear her up. I was anxious to know whether she was alone at Fongueusemare. No, Robert was living with her: Juliette, Édouard, and their children had been spending August with them. We had reached the bench; we sat down and the conversation for a few minutes longer dragged along in the usual commonplace inquiries.

She asked after my work. I replied with a bad grace. I should have liked her to feel that my work no longer interested me. I should have liked to disappoint her as she had disappointed me. I do not know whether I succeeded, but if so, she did not show it. As for me, full of both resentment and love, I did my best to speak as curtly as possible, and was angry with myself for the emotion which at times made my voice tremble.

The setting sun, which had been hidden for a few moments by a cloud, reappeared on the edge of the horizon almost opposite us, flooding the empty fields with a shimmering glory and heaping the narrow valley that opened at our feet with a sudden profusion of wealth; then it disappeared. I sat there dazzled and speechless; I felt that I was wrapped round and steeped in a kind of golden ecstasy, in which my resentment vanished and nothing survived in me but love. Alissa, who had been leaning, drooping against me, sat up; she took out of her bodice a tiny packet wrapped up in tissue paper, made as though she meant to give it me, stopped, seemed to hesitate, and, as I looked at her in surprise:

'Listen, Jerome,' said she, 'this is my amethyst cross that I have here; for the last three evenings I have brought it here because for a long time past I have been wanting to give it you.'

'What am I to do with it?' I asked her, rather brusquely.

'Keep it in memory of me for your daughter.'

'What daughter?' I cried, looking at Alissa without understanding her.

'Please, listen to me quite calmly; no, don't look at me so; don't look at me; it's already difficult enough for me to speak to you; but I must, I simply must say this. Listen, Jerome: one day you will marry – no, don't answer; don't interrupt, I implore you. I only want you to remember that I loved you very much, and . . . a long time ago . . . three years ago I thought that a daughter of yours might one day wear this little cross you liked, in memory of me. Oh! without knowing whose it was . . . and perhaps, too, you might give her . . . my name . . .'

She stopped, her voice choking: I exclaimed, almost with hostility:

'Why not give it her yourself?'

She tried to speak again. Her lips trembled like those of a sobbing child, but she did not cry; the extraordinary light that shone in her eyes flooded her face with an unearthly, an angelic beauty.

'Alissa! whom should I marry? You know I can love no one but you . . .' and suddenly clasping her wildly, almost brutally in my arms, I crushed my kisses on her lips. An instant I held her unresisting, as she half lay back against me; I saw her look grow dim; then her eyes closed, and in a voice so true and melodious that never to my mind will it be equalled:

'Have pity on us, my friend!' she said. 'Oh! don't spoil our love.'

Perhaps she said too: 'Don't be cowardly!' or perhaps it was I who said it to myself; I cannot tell now; but suddenly flinging myself on my knees before her, and folding my arms piously round her:

'If you loved me so, why have you always repulsed me? Think! I waited first for Juliette to be married; I understood your waiting for her to be happy, too; she is happy; you yourself have told me so. I thought for a long time that you didn't want to leave your father; but now we are both alone.'

'Oh! don't let us regret the past,' she murmured. 'I have turned the page now.'

'There is still time, Alissa.'

'No, my friend, there is not time. There was no longer time from the moment when our love made us foresee for one another something better than love. Thanks to you, my friend, my dream climbed so high that any earthly satisfaction would have been a declension. I have often thought of what our life with each other would have been; as soon as it had been less than perfect, I could not have borne . . . our love.'

'Did you ever think what our life would be without each other?'

'No! Never.'

'Now you see! For the last three years, without you, I have been drifting miserably about . . .'

The evening was drawing in.

'I am cold,' said she, getting up and wrapping her shawl too closely round her for me to be able to take her arm again. 'You remember the Scripture text which troubled us so, and which we were afraid we didn't understand properly: "These all received not the promise, God having provided some better thing for us". . . .'

'Do you still believe those words?'

'Indeed I must.'

We walked on for a few moments beside each other, without saying anything more. She went on;

'Can you imagine it, Jerome? – "Some better thing!"'

And suddenly the tears started from her eyes, as she repeated once more: ' "Some better thing!" '

We had again reached the small garden door through which she had come out a little before. She turned towards me;

'Good-bye!' said she. 'No, don't come any further. Good-bye, my beloved friend. Now ... the better thing ... is going to begin.'

One moment she looked at me, at once holding me fast and keeping me at arm's length, her hands on my shoulders, her eyes filled with an unspeakable love.

As soon as the door was shut, as soon as I heard the bolt drawn behind her, I fell against the door, a prey to the extremest despair, and stayed for a long time weeping and sobbing in the night.

But to have kept her, to have forced the door, to have entered by any means whatever into the house, which yet would not have been shut against me – no, even today, when I look back to the past and live it over again – no, it was not possible to me, and whoever does not understand me here, has understood nothing of me up till now.

Intolerable anxiety made me write to Juliette a few days later. I told her of my visit to Fongueusemare, and how much Alissa's paleness and thinness had alarmed me; I implored her to see what could be done, and to give me news which I could no longer expect to get from Alissa herself.

Less than a month later, I received the following letter:

'My dear Jerome,

'This is to give you very sad news; our poor Alissa is no more. Alas! the fears you expressed in your letter were only too well founded. For the last few months, without being ill exactly, she seemed to be wasting away; she yielded, however, to my entreaties and consented to see Dr A—, who wrote to me that there was nothing serious the matter with her. But three days after the visit you paid her, she suddenly left Fongueusemare. It was from a letter of Robert's that I learnt she was gone; she writes to me so seldom that if it had not been for him I should have known nothing of her flight, for I should have been a long time before taking alarm at her silence. I blamed Robert severely for having let her go in this way, and for not having gone with her to Paris. Will you believe that from that moment we were ignorant of her address? You can imagine my sickening anxiety; impossible to see her, impossible even to write to her. Robert, it is true, went to Paris a few days later, but he was unable to discover anything. He is so slack that we could not trust to his taking the proper steps. We had to tell the police; it was not possible to remain in such cruel uncertainty. Édouard then went himself, and at last managed to discover the little nursing home where Alissa had taken refuge. Alas! too late. I received a letter from the head of the home announcing her death, and, at the same time, a telegram from Édouard, who was not in time to see her again. On the last day she had written our address on an envelope, so that we might be told, and in another envelope she had put the copy of a letter she had sent our lawyer at Le Havre containing her last instructions. I think there is a passage in this letter which concerns you: I will let you know soon. Édouard and Robert were able to be present at the funeral which took place the day before yesterday. They were not the only persons to follow the bier. Some of the patients of the nursing home wished to be present at the ceremony and to accompany the body to the cemetery. As for me, I am expecting my fifth baby any day now, and unfortunately I was unable to move.

'My dear Jerome, I know the deep sorrow this loss will cause you, and I write to you with a breaking heart. I have been obliged to stop in bed for the last two days, and I write with difficulty, but I could not let anyone else, not even Édouard or Robert, speak to you of her whom we two, doubtless, were the only persons in the world to know. Now that I am an almost old mother of a family, and that the burning past is covered over with a heap of ashes, I may hope to see you again. If business or pleasure ever takes you to Nîmes, come on to Aigues-Vives. Édouard would be glad to know you, and you and I would be able to talk together of Alissa. Good-bye, my dear Jerome.

'Affectionately and sadly yours . . .'

A few days later, I learnt that Alissa had left Fongueusemare to her brother, but had asked that all things that were in her room and a few pieces of furniture which she mentioned, should be sent to Juliette. I was shortly to receive some papers which she had put in a sealed packet addressed to me. I learnt, also, that she had asked that the little amethyst cross which I had refused at my last visit should be put round her neck, and I heard from Édouard that this had been done.

The sealed packet which the lawyer sent me contained Alissa's journal. I here transcribe a considerable number of its pages. I transcribe them without commentary. You will imagine well enough the reflections I made as I read, and the commotion of my heart, of which I could but give a too imperfect idea.

LEFT Le Havre the day before yesterday; yesterday arrived at Nîmes; my first journey! With no housekeeping to do and no cooking to look after, and consequently with a slight feeling of idleness, today, the 23rd May, 188–, my twenty-fifth birthday, I begin this journal – without much pleasure, a little for the sake of company; for, perhaps for the first time in my life, I feel lonely – in a different, a foreign land almost, one with which I have not yet made acquaintance. It has, no doubt, the same things to say to me as Normandy – the same that I listen to untiringly at Fongueusemare – for God is nowhere different from Himself – but this southern land speaks a language I have not yet heard, and to which I listen wondering.

24th May

Juliette is dozing on a sofa near me – in the open gallery which is the chief charm of the house, built as it is after the Italian fashion. The gallery opens on to the gravelled courtyard which is a continuation of the garden. Without leaving her sofa, Juliette can see the lawn sloping down to the piece of water, where a tribe of parti-coloured ducks disport themselves, and two swans sail. A stream which, they say, never runs dry in the heat of any summer, feeds it and then flows through the garden, which merges into a grove of ever-increasing wildness, more and more shut in by the bed of a dried torrent on the one side and the vineyards on the other, and finally strangled altogether between them.

Édouard Teissières yesterday showed my father the garden, the farm, the cellars, and the vineyards, while I stayed behind with Juliette – so that this morning, while it was still very early, I was able to make my first voyage of discovery in the park, by myself. A great many plants and strange trees, whose names, however, I should have liked to know. I pick a twig of each of them so as to be told what they are, at lunch. In some of them I recognize the evergreen oaks which Jerome admired in the gardens of the Villa Borghese or Doria-Pamfili – so distantly related to our northern tree, of such a different character! Almost at the further end of the park there is a narrow, mysterious glade which they shelter, bending over a carpet of grass so soft to the feet that it seems an invitation to the choir of nymphs. I wonder – I am almost scared that my feeling for nature, which at Fongueusemare is so profoundly Christian, should here become, in spite of myself, half pagan. And yet the kind of awe which oppressed me more and more was religious too. I whispered the words: '*hic nemus*'. The air was crystalline; there was a strange silence. I was thinking of Orpheus, of Armida, when all at once there rose a solitary bird's song, so near me, so pathetic, so pure, that it seemed suddenly as though all nature had been awaiting it. My heart beat violently; I stayed for a moment leaning against a tree, and then came in before anyone was up.

26th May

Still no letter from Jerome. If he had written to me at Le Havre, his letter would have been forwarded. . . . I can confide my anxiety to no one but this book; for the last three days I have not been distracted from it for an instant, either by our excursion yesterday to Les Baux, or by reading, or by prayer. Today I can write of nothing else; the curious melancholy from which I have been suffering ever since I arrived at Aigues-Vives has, perhaps, no other cause – and yet I feel it at such a depth within me that it seems to me now as if it had been there for a long time past, and as if the joy on which I prided myself did no more than cover it over.

27th May

Why should I lie to myself? It is by an effort of mind that

I rejoice in Juliette's happiness. That happiness which I longed for so much, to the extent of offering my own in sacrifice to it, is painful to me, now that I see that she has obtained it without trouble, and that it is so different from what she and I imagined. How complicated it all is! Yes . . . I see well enough that a horrible revival of egoism in me is offended at her having found her happiness elsewhere than in my sacrifice – at her not having needed my sacrifice in order to be happy.

And now I ask myself, as I feel what uneasiness Jerome's silence causes me: Was that sacrifice really- consummated in my heart? I am, as it were, humiliated, to feel that God no longer exacts it. Can it be that I was not equal to it?

28th May

How dangerous this analysis of my sadness is! I am already growing attached to this book. Is my personal vanity, which I thought I had mastered, reasserting its rights here? No; may my soul never use this journal as a flattering mirror before which to attire itself! It is not out of idleness that I write, as I thought at first, but out of sadness. Sadness is a *state of sin*, which had ceased to be mine, which I hate, from whose *complications* I wish to free my soul. This book must help me to find my happiness in myself once more.

Sadness is a complication. I never used to analyse my happiness.

At Fongueusemare I was alone, too, still more alone – why did I not feel it? And when Jerome wrote to me from Italy, I was willing that he should see without me, that he should live without me; I followed him in thought, and out of his joy I made my own. And now, in spite of myself, I want him; without him every new thing I see is irksome to me.

10th June

Long interruption of this journal which I had scarcely begun; birth of little Lise; long hours of watching beside Juliette; I take no pleasure in writing anything here that I can write to Jerome. I should like to keep myself from the intolerable fault which is common to so many women – that of writing too much. Let me consider this notebook as a means of perfection.

There followed several pages of notes made in the course of her reading, extracts, etc. Then, dated from Fongueusemare once more:

16th July

Juliette is happy; she says so, seems so; I have no right, no reason to doubt it. Whence comes this feeling of dissatisfaction, of discomfort, which I have now when I am with her? Perhaps from feeling that such happiness is so practical, so easily obtained, so perfectly 'to measure' that it seems to cramp the soul and stifle it. . . .

And I ask myself now whether it is really happiness that I desire, so much as the progress towards happiness. Oh, Lord! preserve me from a happiness to which I might too easily attain! Teach me to put off my happiness, to place it as far away from me as Thou art.

Several pages here had been torn out; they referred, no doubt, to our painful meeting at Le Havre. The journal did not begin again till the following year; the pages were not dated, but had certainly been written at the time of my stay at Fongueusemare.

Sometimes as I listen to him talking I seem to be watching myself think. He explains me and discovers me to myself. Should I exist without him? I *am* only when I am with him. . . .

Sometimes I hesitate as to whether what I feel for him is really what people call love – the picture that is generally drawn of love is so different from that which I should like to draw. I should like nothing to be said about it, and to love him without knowing that I love him. I should like, above all, to love him without his knowing it.

I no longer get any joy out of that part of life that has to be lived without him. My virtue is all only to please him – and yet, when I am with him, I feel my virtue weakening.

I used to like learning the piano, because it seemed to me that I was able to make some progress in it every day. That too, perhaps, is the secret of the pleasure I take in reading a book in a foreign language; not, indeed, that I prefer any other language whatever to our own, or that the writers I admire in it appear to me in any way inferior to those of other countries – but the slight difficulty that lies in the pursuit of their meaning and feeling, the unconscious pride of overcoming this difficulty, and of overcoming it more and more successfully, adds to my intellectual pleasure a certain spiritual contentment, which it seems to me I cannot do without.

However blessed it might be, I cannot desire a state without progress. I imagine heavenly joy, not as a confounding of the spirit with God, but as an infinite, a perpetual drawing near to Him . . . and if I were not afraid of playing upon words I should say that I did not care for any joy that was not *progressive*.

This morning we were sitting on the bench in the avenue; we were not talking, and did not feel any need to talk. . . . Suddenly he asked me if I believed in a future life.

'Oh! Jerome!' I cried at once, 'it is more than hope I have; it is certainty.'

And it seemed to me, on a sudden, that my whole faith had, as it were, been poured into that exclamation.

'I should like to know,' he added. He stopped a few moments; then: 'Would you act differently without your faith?'

'How can I tell?' I answered; and I added: 'And you, my dear, you yourself, and in spite of yourself, can no longer act otherwise than as if you were inspired by the liveliest faith. And I should not love you if you were different.'

No, Jerome, no, it is not after a future recompense that our virtue is striving; it is not for recompense that our love is seeking. A generous soul is hurt by the idea of being rewarded for its efforts; nor does it consider virtue an adornment: no, virtue is the form of its beauty.

Papa is not so well again; nothing serious, I hope, but he has been obliged to go back to his milk diet for the last three days.

Yesterday evening, Jerome had just gone up to his room; Papa, who was sitting up with me for a little, left me alone for a few minutes. I was sitting on the sofa, or rather – a thing I hardly ever do – I was lying down, I don't know why. The lamp-shade was shading my eyes and the upper part of my body from the light; I was mechanically looking at my feet, which showed a little below my dress in the light thrown upon them by the lamp. When Papa came back, he stood for a few moments at the door, staring at me, oddly, half smiling, half sad. I got up with a vague feeling of shyness; then he called me:

'Come and sit beside me,' said he; and, though it was already late, he began speaking to me about my mother, which he had never done since their separation. He told me how he had married her, how much he had loved her, and how much she had at first been to him.

'Papa,' I said to him at last, 'do, please, say why you are telling me this this evening – what makes you tell me this just this particular evening?'

'Because, just now, when I came into the drawing-room and saw you lying on the sofa, I thought for a moment it was your mother.'

The reason I asked this so insistently was because that very evening Jerome was reading over my shoulder, standing leaning over me. I could not see him, but I felt his breath and, as it were, the warmth and pulsation of his body. I pretended to go on reading, but my mind had stopped working; I could not even distinguish the lines; a perturbation so strange took possession of me that I was obliged to get up from my chair quickly, whilst I still could; I managed to leave the room for a few minutes, luckily without his noticing anything. But a little later, when I was alone in the drawing-room and lay down on the sofa, where Papa thought I looked like my mother, at that very moment I was thinking of her.

I slept very badly last night; I was disturbed, oppressed, miserable, haunted by the recollection of the past, which came over me like a wave of remorse.

Lord, teach me the horror of all that has any appearance of evil.

Poor Jerome! If he only knew that sometimes he would have but a single sign to make, and that sometimes I wait for him to make it. . . .

When I was a child, even then it was because of him that I wanted to be beautiful. It seems to me now that I have never striven after perfection, except for him. And that this perfection can only be attained without him, is of all Thy teachings, my God! the one that is most disconcerting to my soul.

How happy must that soul be for whom virtue is one with love! Sometimes I doubt whether there is any other virtue than love . . . to love as much as possible and continually more and more. . . . But at other times, alas! virtue appears to me to be nothing but resistance to love. What! shall I dare to call that virtue which is the most natural inclination of my heart? Oh, tempting sophism! Specious allurement! Cunning mirage of happiness!

This morning I read in La Bruyère:

'In the course of this life one sometimes meets with pleasures so dear, promises so tender, which are yet forbidden us, that it is natural to desire at least that they might be permitted; charms so great can be surpassed only when virtue teaches us to renounce them.'

Why did I invent here that there was anything forbidden? Can it be that I am secretly attracted by a charm more powerful and a sweetness greater still than that of love? Oh! that it were possible to carry our own souls forward together, by force of love, beyond love!

Alas! I understand now only too well; between God and him there is no other obstacle but myself. If perhaps, as he says, his love for me at first inclined him to God, now that very love hinders him; he lingers with me, prefers me, and I am become the idol that keeps him back from making further progress in virtue. One of us two must needs attain to it; and as I despair of overcoming the love in my coward heart, grant me, my God, vouchsafe me strength to teach him to love me no longer, so that at the cost of my merits I may bring Thee his, which are so infinitely preferable . . . and if today my soul sobs with grief at losing him, do I not lose him to find him again hereafter in Thee?

Tell me, oh, my God! what soul ever deserved Thee more? Was he not born for something better than to love me? And should I love him so much if he were to stop short at myself? How much all that might become heroic dwindles in the midst of happiness!

Sunday

'God having provided some better thing for us.'

Monday 3rd May

To think that happiness is here, close by, offering itself, and that one only has to put out one's hand to grasp it . . .

This morning, as I was talking to him, I consummated the sacrifice.

Monday evening

He leaves tomorrow. . . .

Dear Jerome, I still love you with infinite tenderness; but never more shall I be able to tell you so. The constraint which I lay upon my eyes, upon my lips, upon my soul, is so hard that to leave you is a relief and a bitter satisfaction.

I strive to act according to reason, but at the moment of action the reasons which make me act escape me, or appear foolish; I no longer believe in them.

The reasons which make me fly from him? I no longer believe in them . . . . And yet I fly from him, sadly and without understanding why I fly.

Lord! that we might advance towards Thee, Jerome and I together, each beside the other, each helping the other; that we might walk along the way of life like two pilgrims, of whom one says at times to the other: 'Lean on me, brother, if you are weary,' and to whom the other replies: 'It is enough to feel you near me. . .' But no! The way Thou teachest, Lord, is a narrow way – so narrow that two cannot walk in it abreast.

5th July

More than six weeks have gone by without my opening this book. Last month, as I was re-reading some of its pages, I became aware of a foolish, wicked anxiety to write well . . . which I owe to *him*. . . .

As though in this book, which I began only so as to help myself to do without *him*, I was continuing to write to *him*.

I have torn up all the pages which seemed to me to be *well written*. (I know what I mean by this.) I ought to have torn up all those in which there was any question of him. I ought to have torn them all up, I could not.

And already, because I tore up those few pages, I had a little feeling of pride . . . . a pride which I should laugh at if my heart were not so sick.

It really seemed as though I had done something meritorious, and as though what I had destroyed had been of some importance!

6th July

I have been obliged to banish from my bookshelves . . .

I fly from him in one book only to find him in another. I hear his voice reading me even those pages which I discover without him. I care only for what interests him, and my mind has taken the form of his to such an extent, that I can distin-

guish one from the other no better than I did at the time when
I took pleasure in feeling they were one.

Sometimes I force myself to write badly in order to escape
from the rhythm of his phrases; but even to struggle against
him is still to be concerned with him. I have made a resolution
to read nothing but the Bible (perhaps the *Imitation*), and to
write nothing more in this book, except every evening the
chief text of my reading.

There followed a kind of diary, in which the date of each day,
starting with July 1st, was accompanied by a text. I transcribe only
those which are accompanied by some commentary.

20th July

'Sell all that thou hast and give it to the poor.'

I understand that I ought to give to the poor this heart of
mine which belongs only to Jerome. And by so doing should
I not teach him at the same time to do likewise? . . . Lord, grant
me this courage.

24th July

I have stopped reading the *Interior Consolation*. The old-
fashioned language greatly charmed me, but it was distracting,
and the almost pagan joy it gives me is far removed from the
edification which I set myself to get from it.

I have taken up the *Imitation* again and not even in the Latin
text, which I was vain of understanding. I am glad that the
translation in which I read it should not even be signed. It is
true it is Protestant, but 'adapted to the use of all Christian
communities,' says the title.

'Oh, if thou wert sensible how much peace thou wouldest
procure for thyself and joy for others, by rightly ordering
thyself, methinks thou wouldest be more solicitous for thy
spiritual progress!'

10th August

If I were to cry to Thee, my God, with the impulsive faith of a child and with the heavenly tongues of angels. . . .

All this comes to me, I know, not from Jerome, but from Thee.

Why, then, between Thee and me, dost Thou everywhere set his image?

14th August

Only two months more in which to complete my work . . . Oh, Lord, grant me Thy help!

20th August

I feel – I feel by my *unhappiness* that the sacrifice is not consummated in my heart. My God, grant that henceforth I owe to none but Thee the joy that he alone used to give me.

28th August

How mediocre and miserable is the virtue to which I attain! Do I then exact too much from myself? . . . To suffer no more.

What cowardice makes me continually implore God for His strength? My prayers now are nothing but complainings.

29th August

'Consider the lilies of the field . . .'

This simple saying plunged me this morning into a sadness from which nothing could distract me. I went out into the country and these words, which I kept continually repeating to myself, filled my heart and eyes with tears. I contemplated the vast and empty plain where the labourer was toiling, bent over his plough. . . . 'The lilies of the field . . .' But, Lord, where are they . . .?

16th September, 10 o'clock at night

I have seen him again. He is here under this roof. I see the light from his window shining on the grass. He is still up as I write these lines, and perhaps he is thinking of me. He has not changed. He says so and I feel it. Shall I be able to show myself to him such as I have resolved to be, so that his love may disown me?

24th September

Oh, torturing conversation in which I succeeded in feigning indifference – coldness, when my heart was fainting within me! Up till now I had contented myself with avoiding him. This morning I was able to believe that God would give me strength to be victorious and that to slink for ever out of the combat was to prove myself a coward. Did I triumph? Does Jerome love me a little less? Alas! I both hope and fear it together. I have never loved him more.

And if it is Thy will, Lord, that to save him from me I must compass my own perdition, so be it.

'Enter into my heart and into my soul in order to bear in them my sufferings and to continue to ensure in me what remains to Thee to suffer of Thy Passion.'

We spoke of Pascal . . . What did I say? What shameful foolish words? I suffered even as I uttered them, but tonight I repent them as a blasphemy. I turned again to the heavy volume of the *Pensées*, which opened of itself at this passage in the letters to Mademoiselle de Roannez:

'We do not feel our bonds as long as we follow willingly him who leads; but as soon as we begin to resist and to draw away, then indeed we suffer.'

These words affected me so personally that I did not have strength to go on reading, but opening the book in another place I came across an admirable passage which I did not know and which I have just copied out.

The first volume of the Journal came to an end here. No doubt the next had been destroyed, for in the papers which Alissa left behind the Journal did not begin again till three years later – still at Fongueusemare – in September – a short time, that is to say, before our last meeting.

The last volume begins with the sentences which follow.

17th September

My God, Thou knowest I have need of him to love Thee.

20th September

My God, give him to me so that I may give Thee my heart.
My God, let me see him only once more.
My God, I engage to give Thee my heart. Grant me what my love beseeches. I will give what remains to me of life to Thee alone.
My God, forgive me this despicable prayer, but I cannot keep his name from my lips nor forget the anguish of my heart.
My God, I cry to Thee. Do not forsake me in my distress.

21st September

'Whatever ye shall ask the Father in my name . . .'
Lord, in Thy name, I dare not.
But though I no longer formulate my prayer, wilt Thou be the less aware of the delirious longing of my heart?

27th September

Ever since the morning a great calm. Spent nearly the whole night in meditation, in prayer. Suddenly I was conscious of a kind of luminous peace like the imagination I had as a child of the Holy Ghost: it seemed to wrap me round, to descend into me. I went to bed at once fearing that my joy was due only to nervous exaltation. I went to sleep fairly quickly without this felicity leaving me. It is still here this morning in all its completeness. I have the certainty now that he will come.

30th September

Jerome, my friend! you whom I still call brother, but whom I love infinitely more than a brother ... How many times I have cried your name in the beech copse! Every evening towards dusk I go out by the little gate of the kitchen-garden and walk down the avenue where it is already dark. If you were suddenly to answer me, if you were to appear there from behind the stony bank round which I so eagerly seek you, or if I were to see you in the distance, seated on the bench waiting for me, my heart would not leap ... no! I am astonished at not seeing you.

1st October

Nothing yet. The sun has set in a sky of incomparable purity. I am waiting. I know that soon I shall be sitting with him on this very bench. I hear his voice already. I like it so much when he says my name. He will be here! I shall put my hand in his hand. I shall let my head lean on his shoulder. I shall breathe beside him. Yesterday I brought out some of his letters with me to re-read, but I did not look at them – I was too much taken up with the thought of him. I took with me, too, the amethyst cross he used to like and which I used to wear one summer every evening as long as I did not want him to go. I should like to give him this cross. For a long time past I have had a dream – that he was married and I godmother to his first daughter, a little Alissa, to whom I gave this ornament. ... Why have I never dared tell him?

2nd October

My soul today is as light and joyful as a bird would be that had made its nest in the sky. For today he will come. I feel it! I know it! I should like to proclaim it aloud to the world. I feel I must write it here. I cannot hide my joy any longer. Even Robert, who is usually so inattentive and indifferent to what concerns me, noticed it. His questions embarrassed me and I did not know what to answer. How shall I be able to wait till this evening? . . .

Some kind of strange transparent bandage over my eyes seems to show me his image everywhere – his image magnified, and all love's rays are concentrated on a single burning spot in my heart.

Oh! how this waiting tires me!

Lord, unclose for me one moment the wide gateways of gladness.

3rd October

All is over. Alas! he has slipped out of my arms like a shadow. He was here! He was here! I feel him still. I call him. My hands, my lips seek him in vain in the night. . . .

I can neither pray nor sleep. I went out again into the dark garden. I was afraid – in my room – everywhere in the house – I was afraid. My anguish brought me once more to the door behind which I had left him. I opened it with a mad hope that he might have come back. I called. I groped in the darkness. I have come in again to write to him. I cannot accept my grief.

What has happened? What did I say to him? What did I do? Why do I always want to exaggerate my virtue to him? What can be the worth of a virtue which my whole heart denies? I was secretly false to the words which God set upon my lips. In spite of all that my heart was bursting with, I could bring nothing out. Jerome! Jerome, my unhappy friend in whose presence my heart bleeds and in whose absence I perish, believe nothing of all I said to you just now, but the words spoken by my love.

Tore up my letter, then wrote again. . . . Here is the dawn, grey, wet with tears, as sad as my thoughts. I hear the first sounds of the farm and everything that was sleeping re-awakens to life. . . . 'Arise, now. The hour is at hand. . . .'

My letter shall not go.

5th October

Oh, jealous God, who hast despoiled me, take Thou possession of my heart. All warmth henceforth has forsaken it; nothing will touch it more. Help me to triumph over the melancholy remnant of myself. This house, this garden encourage my love intolerably. I must fly to some place where I shall see none but Thee.

Thou wilt help me to bestow upon Thy poor what fortune I possessed; let me leave Fongueusemare, which I cannot dispose of easily, to Robert. I have made my will, it is true, but I am ignorant of the necessary formalities and yesterday I could not talk to the lawyer properly, as I was afraid he might suspect the decision I had taken and warn Juliette and Robert. I will finish this business in Paris.

10th October

Arrived here so tired that I was obliged to stay in bed the first two days. The doctor, who was sent for against my will, speaks of an operation which he considers necessary. What is the use of objecting? But I easily made him believe that I was frightened at the idea of an operation and preferred waiting till I had 'regained my strength a little'.

I have managed to conceal my name and address. I have deposited enough money with the management of the house for them to make no difficulty about taking me in and keeping me for as long as God shall continue to think it necessary.

I like this room. The walls need no other decoration than their perfect cleanliness. I was quite astonished to feel almost joyful. The reason is that I expect nothing more from life – that I must be content now with God, and His love is sweet only if it fills to completion whatever space there is within us. . . .

The only book I have brought with me is the Bible: but today there sounded in me louder than any words I find there, this wild and passionate sob of Pascal's: 'Whatever is not God cannot satisfy my longing.'

Oh! too human joy, that my imprudent heart desired! . . . Was it to wring this cry from me, Lord, that Thou hast thus bereft me?

12th October

Thy Kingdom come! May it come in me; so that Thou alone mayest reign over me and reign over the whole of me. I will no longer grudge Thee my heart.

Though I am as tired as if I were very old, my soul keeps a strange childishness. I am still the little girl, who could not go to sleep before everything in her room was tidy and the clothes she had taken off neatly folded beside her bed. . . . That is how I should like to get ready to die.

13th October

Re-read my journal before destroying it. 'It is unworthy of noble natures to spread round them the disturbance they feel.' It is, I think, Clotilde de Vaux who says this so finely.

Just as I was going to throw this journal into the fire, I felt a kind of warning which held me back. It seemed to me that it no longer belonged to me, that I had no right to deprive Jerome of it, that I had never written it except for him. My anxieties, my doubts seem to me now so foolish that I can no longer attach any importance to them, or believe that they will disturb Jerome. My God, grant that he may at times catch in these lines the unskilled accent of a heart, passionately desirous of urging him to those heights of virtue which I myself despaired of reaching.

'My God, lead me to the rock that is higher than I.'

15th October

'Joy, joy, joy, tears of joy . . .'*

* Quotation from Pascal. (*Translator's note*)

Above human joy and beyond all suffering, yes, I foresee that radiant joy. The 'rock that is higher than I' bears, I know, the name of happiness . . . I understand that my whole life has been vain, except in so far as it culminates in happiness. . . . Ah! Lord, but Thy promise to the pure and renouncing soul was this: 'Blessed *from henceforth*' said Thy holy word, 'Blessed are they which die in the Lord from henceforth.' Must I wait until I die? This is the point where my faith wavers. Lord! I cry unto Thee with all my strength. I am in the night! I am waiting for the dawn. I cry unto Thee with a crying that wastes me to death. Come and slake the thirst of my heart. It is now, at once, that I thirst for happiness. . . . Or ought I to persuade myself that I have it? And as the pipe of the impatient bird before daybreak calls rather than heralds the light, ought I to sing, without waiting for the night to dwindle?

16th October

Jerome, I wish I could teach you perfect joy.

This morning I was shattered by a fit of sickness. And afterwards I felt so weak that for a moment I hoped I was going to die. But no; first a great calm fell upon my whole being; then a pang of anguish pierced me, a shudder of my flesh and soul; it was like the sudden and disenchanting *illumination* of my life. It seemed to me that I saw for the first time the walls of my room in their atrocious bareness. I was seized with fear. Even now I am writing to reassure myself, to calm myself. O Lord! may I reach the end without blasphemy!

I was able to get up again. I went down on my knees like a child. . . .

I should like to die now, quickly, before again realizing that I am alone.

*

I SAW Juliette again last year. More than ten years had gone by since her last letter, in which she told me of Alissa's death. A journey to Provence gave me an opportunity of stopping at Nîmes. The Teissières occupy an important house in the Avenue de Feuchères, in a noisy and central part of the town. Although I had written to announce my arrival, it was with considerable emotion that I crossed the threshold.

A maidservant showed me into the drawing-room, where Juliette joined me in a few minutes. I thought I saw Aunt Plantier – the same gait, the same stoutness, the same breathless hospitality. She immediately began plying me with questions (without waiting for my answers) as to my career, my manner of living in Paris, my occupations, my acquaintances; what was my business in the South? Why shouldn't I go on to Aigues-Vives, where Edouard would be so happy to see me? ... Then she gave me news of all the family, talked of her husband, her children, her brother, of the last vintage, of the autumn prices. ... I learnt that Robert had sold Fongueusemare in order to live at Aigues-Vives: that he was now Édouard's partner, which left her husband free to travel, and in particular to look after the commercial side of the business, whilst Robert stayed on the land, improving and increasing the plantations.

In the meantime I was uneasily looking round for anything that might recall the past. I recognized, indeed, amongst the otherwise new furniture of the drawing-room, certain pieces that came from Fongueusemare; but of the past which was quivering within me, Juliette now seemed to be oblivious, or else to be endeavouring to distract our thoughts from it.

Two boys of twelve and thirteen were playing on the stairs; she called them in to introduce them to me. Lise, the eldest of her children, had gone with her father to Aigues-Vives. Another boy of ten was expected in from his walk; it was he whose advent Juliette had told me of in the same letter in which she had announced our bereavement. There had been some trouble over this last confinement; Juliette had suffered from its effects for a long time; then last year, as an afterthought, she had given birth to a little girl, whom, to hear her talk, she preferred to all her other children.

'My room, where she sleeps, is next door,' said she; 'come and see her.' And as I was following her: 'Jerome, I didn't dare write to you . . . would you consent to be the baby's god-father?

'Yes, with pleasure, if you would like me to,' said I, slightly surprised, as I bent over the cradle. 'What is my god-daughter's name?'

'Alissa . . .' replied Juliette, in a whisper. 'She is a little like her, don't you think so?'

I pressed Juliette's hand, without answering. Little Alissa, whom her mother lifted, opened her eyes; I took her in my arms.

'What a good father you would make!' said Juliette, trying to laugh. 'What are you waiting for to marry?'

'To have forgotten a great many things,' I replied, and watched her blush.

'Which you are hoping to forget soon?'

'Which I do not hope ever to forget.'

'Come in here,' said she, abruptly, leading the way into a smaller room, which was already dark, and of which one door led into her bedroom, and another into the drawing-room. 'This is where I take refuge when I have a moment to myself; it is the quietest room in the house; I feel that I am almost sheltered from life in here.'

The window of this small drawing-room did not open, like those of the other rooms, on to the noises of the town, but on to a sort of courtyard planted with trees.

'Let us sit down,' said she, dropping into an armchair. 'If I understood you rightly it is to Alissa's memory that you mean to remain faithful.'

I stayed a moment without answering.

'Rather, perhaps, to her idea of me. No, don't give me any credit for it. I think I couldn't do otherwise. If I married another woman, I could only pretend to love her.'

'Ah!' said she, as though indifferently, then turning her face away from me, she bent it towards the ground, as if she were looking for something she had lost. 'Then you think that one can keep a hopeless love in one's heart for so long as that?'

'Yes, Juliette.'

'And that life can breathe upon it every day, without extinguishing it?'

The evening came slowly up like a grey tide, reaching and flooding each object which seemed to come to life again in the gloom and repeat in a whisper the story of its past. Once more I saw Alissa's room, all the furniture of which Juliette had collected together here. And then she turned her face towards me again, but it was too dark for me to distinguish her features, so that I did not know whether her eyes were shut or not. I thought her very beautiful. And we both now remained without speaking.

'Come!' said she at last: 'we must wake up.'

I saw her rise, take a step forward, drop again, as though she had no strength, into the nearest chair; she put her hands up to her face and I thought I saw that she was crying.

A servant came in, bringing the lamp.